U.N.C.L.E.

THE MAN
FROM
U.N.C.L.E.

THE
DOOMSDAY
AFFAIR

THE MAN
FROM
U.N.C.L.E.

THE
DOOMSDAY
AFFAIR

HARRY
WHITTINGTON

Based on the
cult TV spy series

B🌳XTREE

Published in the UK 1993 by
BOXTREE LIMITED
Broadwall House
21 Broadwall
London SE1 9PL

First published in the UK 1965 by Souvenir Press in
association with The New English Library.

First published in the USA 1965 by Ace Books Inc.

10 9 8 7 6 5 4 3 2 1

Cover photograph courtesy of The Kobal Collection.
Cover design by Head Design.

Typesetting by DP Photosetting, Aylesbury, Bucks.
Printed and bound by Cox & Wyman Ltd, Reading, Berkshire.

ISBN: 1 85283 882 5

A catalogue record for this book is available from the British
Library.

Contents

PART ONE
INCIDENT IN PINK HAWAII   **7**

PART TWO
INCIDENT AT THE HUNGRY PUSSYCAT   **51**

PART THREE
INTERLUDE IN BEDLAM   **101**

PART FOUR
**INCIDENT THE MORNING AFTER
   DOOMSDAY**   **129**

PART ONE

INCIDENT IN PINK HAWAII

I

AN INSTANT BEFORE, she had been alive.

One moment she was laughing, so darkly lovely that she'd ignite a faraway look in any man's eyes. Simply being in the same room with her could be an unnerving experience, yet she'd been anxious to unburden herself, frightened, troubled, wanting to get down to the serious business of a confidential talk with Solo on the subject of a mutual enemy.

'Let me get out of this lei and into something more comfortable,' was what she'd said. And then abruptly she was dead.

Napoleon Solo stood immobile, staring at the bewitching corpse without a face. He swallowed hard, thinking she was the loveliest corpse between where she lay on the pink shag rug – and eternity.

For this moment checkmated by shock, he caught a glimpse of himself in the pink mirror. Deceptively slender, no more than of medium height, he had the smart appearance of a young interne, a Madison Avenue account exec, a youthful professional man swinging his way through the fabled gay-pads of the globe. He looked like anything except what he was: a diamond-hard, exhaustively-trained enforcement agent for perhaps the most important secret service in the

7

world, the United Network Command for Law and Enforcement.

His smile was easy, distilled of a genuine warmth and an inner glow of a healthy, fine-honed body. His jacket and slacks were impeccably tailored with a Brooks Brothers quality, but the disarming cut concealed a strapped-down Berns-Martin shoulder holster housing its hidden U.N.C.L.E. Special, thirty-seven ounces of deadly weapon, including silencer.

Solo shook his head, stunned, even while a substantial fragment of his precision-trained intellect warned him that he could join her in eternity in the seconds it was costing him to recover from the horror and outrage of her murder. He'd encountered sudden death often, in his work with U.N.C.L.E., but this girl was so young, so lovely – and so abruptly mutilated.

He glanced at the gold face of his Accutron watch, mechanically noting the time. Time no longer had meaning for Ursula, but he still operated for an agency where time was forever of the essence.

A faint breeze faltered in hesitant curiosity in the pink window drapes. The fabric bent inward gently and then expired against the full-length windows as if the breeze had darted in terror back out to the sandy beach which lay like stained carpeting between the pink hotel and the incredible blue of the sea.

Solo broke the spell at last, stepped forward and bent down beside the dead girl.

He scraped his fingers over the rug, attempting to assemble the atoms of flowers and string that had recently been a lei of ginger flowers tossed over Ursula's head in a laughing *Aloha* at the Honolulu International Airport less than an hour ago.

Solo shook his head again, refusing to accept it. Murder from a lei?

He scowled. *Aloha* meant both hello *and* goodbye. Hail and farewell. So long, Ursula. She'd reached up with those golden arms to remove the lei over her head

8

and the mechanism concealed in the bright ginger flowers had blown her face away. There had not even been time for her to cry out, or for Solo to reach her from across the pink bed.

Solo straightened up, shaking off the horror of her sudden and brutal death. It was as if someone compounded of evil had searched diligently to find the most heartless manner of death for lovely Ursula Baynes-Neefirth. She was vain about that classic perfection of her delicately hewn face. Blow it away, then. They'll seal her casket and sew her in a shroud.

He warned himself for the last time that emotionalism in his job was taboo because it softened him, strangled his thought processes, rendering him ineffective to his profession and to himself.

In the next instant, Solo began to move efficiently, as if unaware of the corpse on the pink carpeting.

From his attaché case he drew a small chrome, plastic and metal rectangle that fitted snugly in his palm. From an upper edge he pulled two thread-like antennae that trembled reel-like in the scented breeze in from the banyan park.

He pressed a button on the sender-set, blew into the golden netted speaker, waited a moment and then spoke slowly, enunciating clearly: 'Bubba. This is Sonny. Acknowledge. Mayday. Acknowledge, please.'

He pressed a second button and stood staring, his eyes fixed on the beach without seeing it. Waikiki was loud with laughter, bright with bikinis, busy with surfboards and children building castles in the sand. The sea lay milk-blue with the sun shimmering on it.

And in the midst of all this pleasure he was concerned with death.

Death and failure. Ursula's death. His own failure. More than a lovely girl had blown up when that ginger-lei had exploded.

From where does death always strike? From the most innocent-appearing sources of all. A lei of ginger flowers had erupted in violent murder and his chance to find Tixe Ylno had gone in that sudden flash of time.

He grimaced. You got in a place like this, a pink resort hotel in an unreal Pacific vacationland, and you relaxed. And death struck. And failure. It was over, and months of intensive preparation was fragmented like the petals of those ginger flowers.

'Sonny. This is Bubba. Acknowledging. Over.' It was Illya's voice, and he felt a sense of relief.

The small sender–receiver in his hand crackled and then was still. Solo prowled the room, counting, and then he crossed to the corridor door, listened a moment and opened it.

Illya Kuryakin grinned at him from beneath a thatch of golden hair. A slender Slavic type, his enigmatic smiling hid all his emotions and thoughts. Congenitally a loner, he was clever and physically adept; Solo had learned that Illya was a good man to have at his side in a tight spot. It was easy to think that Illya was like a machine, computing danger and finding solutions for it, fashioned for this specific purpose. Sometimes nothing seemed to exist for him but the task assigned to him. Of Russian origin, Illya had worked behind the Iron Curtain – sometimes with the knowledge and consent of the authorities, and, when necessary, without it. He'd trained himself to move fast and never to look back because he'd learned the unpleasant way that the devil takes the man who is caught.

At the moment, Illya wore the smartly crisp uniform of a hotel bellhop, and for all the expression in his high-planed face he might well have had no interest in this world except the size of his anticipated tip.

He said, 'You mentioned Mayday.'

Solo spoke flatly: 'She's dead.'

Illya pushed by him, entering the room. He stood for a full second staring at the lovely body, the faceless corpse. He shook his head.

'A lei,' Solo said.

10

'What?' Kuryakin spun on his heel.

'She was pulling it over her head. Some kind of mechanism. It blew to bits, along with everything else. It was like a Chinese firecracker, then there was this blast of air – the vacuum. It was all over before I could move.'

Illya straightened. 'Who sold her the lei?'

Solo frowned, remembering. 'No one *sold* it to her. It was thrown over her head. A lot of laughter – from a well-wisher. I heard that much.'

'Who put it over her head?'

Solo removed a cigarette lighter from his pocket, flicked it so the fire flared.

He extended the lighter to Illya. 'She's on here, whoever it was. The moment I heard that well-wishing, no-charge bit, I lit a cigarette and snapped her picture. You might want to print them; you're on the roll, in all your bellhop glory.'

Illya nodded, took three small black plastic cups from Solo's attaché bag. He tore open foil sacks of powder developer and setting chemical, added water from the bathroom tap in the three cups.

He broke open the cigarette-lighter camera and inserted the protected film roll into the first cup. The protective skin over the film dissolved on contact with the liquid.

Working, Illya spoke over his shoulder. 'What did you learn from her?'

Solo shook his head. 'Nothing. She was scared.'

'We already knew that.'

'I tried to get her to relax.'

'Three months,' Illya said. 'Shot.'

'Never mind beating me over the head with it.'

'I'm not blaming you.'

'Maybe I'm blaming myself.'

'She was a spy. She was trying to quit Thrush. She must have known better. Why should she think she could make it?'

'I promised her.'

11

'Nobody's perfect.'

'Whoever planned to kill her had it arranged well in advance–'

'That's for sure. No one knew she was meeting you here except the two of us, Waverly, and the man from the President's staff.'

'Somebody knew it.'

Solo prowled the room, turning this over in his mind.

Kuryakin continued working and none of what he must have been thinking showed in his flat, impassive face.

'Somebody knew where Ursula was going to be, and where, when and how to bypass her fears, her instinct for preservation, her caution – and mine!' Solo spread his hands. 'It takes its own kind of intellect to come up with a scheme so simple, and so foolproof.'

Abruptly Solo stopped talking and strode across the room to the baggage rack where the single beige Samsonite weekender bag had rested since the bellhop placed it there when he came into this room with Ursula. The clatter of their relaxed voices still clamoured in his brain.

He reached for the bag and withdrew his hands at the precise instant Illya spoke warningly from the bathroom door: 'Watch it!'

They stared at each other and Solo gave Illya a sombre caricature of a smile.

'You're all systems go again,' Kuryakin assured him with a faint grin.

Solo strode to his attaché case, returned with a handheld explosive-detector. He ran it across the case, along its sides. Gently he turned the weekender over and repeated the process without getting a reaction from the minute needle.

He tossed the detector to Illya, who returned it casually to the attaché case.

Solo released the catches and opened the case. He started into it, not speaking. After a moment he was aware of Illya beside him, as speechless.

Inside the suitcase were two objects; otherwise it was bare. There was a letter addressed to Ursula Neefirth, King's Hotel, Nassau, Bahamas. There was no return address, but the cancellation showed San Francisco, 2 P.M., July 12. Beside the letter, carefully coiled, was a silver whip that glittered when it caught the errant rays of the sun.

Solo opened the envelope, removed the single sheet of cheap typing paper. He unfolded it and held it so that both he and Illya could scan it.

'Meaningless,' Illya said.

'If it's a code, it's their own private make,' Solo said.

'The whip?' Illya said. 'Does this register?'

Solo frowned, aware of the tail-end of a thought flashing through the deep crannies of his mind, darting, but landing nowhere. There was a meaning to the whip, something that had been revealed to them in the briefing on Ursula Baynes-Neefirth at the New York head-quarters of U.N.C.L.E.

'It'll come to me,' he said coldly. 'It's got to.'

Illya glanced at his watch. 'Meantime, it's been thirty minutes up here.'

'All right.'

Solo loosened his tie, unbuttoned his shirt and, in the same downward movement, unbuckled his belt, un-zipped his trousers and stepped out of them.

At the same time, Illya was removing his bellhop's uniform. They exchanged clothing with maximum speed and efficiency.

Illya checked his watch again. 'When you've been out of here for five minutes, I'll call the police and notify the desk – before I walk out ... And don't forget to use the service elevator, will you?'

Solo donned the bellhop uniform. With the trousers on, he crossed the room, returning from the bathroom with the strip of developed film. Drying it beneath the light for a moment, he held the strip under a magnifying

13

glass, scanning along it.

'There she is,' he said. 'Looks like a Chinese doll, doesn't she? A real little death doll.'

II

EVEN IN THE FLESH, the flower girl looked like a doll.

Solo found her in the terminal building at the Honolulu Airport.

He moved through the crowds, thinking how easy it had been. The only delay had been in changing from the bellhop uniform into jacket and slacks in the men's room at Kapiolani Park. Carrying his attaché case, he had returned to his rented Chevvy and crossed town, going directly out to the airfield.

The look of her was the sharpest image in his mind.

And suddenly he had seen her, exactly as if she had stepped from the snapshot.

He paused a moment, and then strode towards her. There were other girls around her, all colourfully dressed in muumuus or draped in holukus, brightly printed with flowers. But the Chinese girl stood out from them as if she were alone.

She wasn't quite five feet tall but her figure and everything else about her was perfect: the delicate China skin, the black hair worn straight, starched and ironed almost to her shoulders. She looked as thought if you turned a key in her back she'd say, 'mama' or 'daddy'.

He sidled through laughing groups, delightfully working his eyes back and forth over her, finding her more elegant than the gay strings of leis on her arm.

And then he remembered the lei she'd thrown over Ursula's head, and some of the beauty of her faded.

The impact of his unwavering gaze somehow communicated itself to the Chinese doll.

Solo saw her head jerk up, her almond eyes, black and frightened suddenly, recognizing him. Fear seeped down from her eyes and her lips parted.

She shook her head.

Solo walked faster.

She turned, looking around like a small, trapped animal. Then she brought her gaze back to Solo's face.

She looked ill. She reached out futilely towards the girl nearest her, then changed her mind and did not speak to her after all. Instead, she dropped the leis from her arm, pushed between the girls in front of her and ran towards the exits.

The girls turned, chattering like mynah birds, calling after her, some of them laughing.

Solo changed his course, tacking hard right towards the doors and the street.

'Look where you're going, young man!'

A stout woman had caught his arm and was shaking it with vigorous disapproval.

Far ahead, he saw the girl's darting run. She went racing past startled people. He tried to follow her with his eyes, but then he had to bring his attention back to the woman who was shaking him, and to the women around them. There were a dozen of them, none under sixty, all being shepherded by a uniformed island guide.

Solo apologized, trying to push his way through them. They all wore leis, carried straw plunder bags and wore comfortable shoes. Clearly they were on an all-expense tour straight from the midwest.

'I beg your pardon,' Solo said, trying to look at the woman grasping his arm and yet not lose sight of the girl who flitted like a sparrow in the sun beyond the doors. 'I'm sorry.'

'What's your hurry, young man? Why don't you look where you're going?' the woman said.

'Make him stay after school, Esther!' one of the other women laughed.

Reminded that she was not in the corridors of her school, the large woman released Solo's arm, flushing slightly. She said again, 'You should look where you're

15

going.'

Solo nodded, trying to step through them and the confusion they created. They milled around him and the bronze-skinned guide like sheep, all bleating at once.

He managed to reach the brink of the flock and he backed away, still nodding, but headed towards the street exits again.

'Look out!'

The woman and her French poodle yelped at the same instant. Solo stopped cold, turning.

She was as tall as Solo in her spike heels. She was metallically sleek from her stockings to her hat, as if her beauty were something anodized upon some long-submerged framework.

He found himself startled because she was all in pink, and the carefully trimmed poodle was dyed a matching pink. The colour brought back the room in the hotel at Waikiki, and the dead girl.

He stepped around the pink, yapping dog, aware that the herd of women was milling around, bleating towards him again.

He ran for the doors. He went through them, but the delay had given the China doll all the time she needed to elude him.

He stopped on the sun-bright pavement, looking around. Cars were lined in the parking area. He brought his gaze back to the pavement. The girl was gone. He had lost her.

Solo stood unmoving for a moment. The sharp pop of a starting motorcycle snagged his attention and he heeled around towards it.

The cycle missed, caught, and smoke flared. The cycle raced out from between two cars, coming directly towards Solo and the exit of the airport.

Solo stepped forward, seeing the bright muumuu of the China doll behind the cycle operator. The boy wore a gaudy purple and yellow shirt and skin tight pants. His thick black hair was cropped close to his skull. His

16

ancestry was a wild mixture of Hawaiian, Chinese, Polynesian. He was stocky, keg-chested, shoulders bunched with muscles, a bull neck, thick lips, a flat wide nose, black eyes under thick brows, a narrow forehead.

The girl clung to the boy, both her arms locked around his stout midriff.

Solo moved out, trying to slow them down. He saw the boy lower his head, feeding gas to the machine. It popped loudly and raced past him.

Solo leaped back to the curb.

He wasted no time trying to figure their direction. The flower girl and her beach boy had only one idea, getting out of here.

Solo ran to the rented car and leaped into it.

He came out on the road and far ahead of him he saw the motorcycle swing out on Dillingham Boulevard without slowing down. The screech of brakes, the protecting clatter of horns struck at him.

He settled down to the business of driving and attempting to keep the reckless cyclist in sight. The small vehicle bounced along the inside lane, cut in between speeding cars. They passed the Oahu prison and sped across the Kapalama drainage canal into downtown Honolulu.

Brakes screeched as the cycle went left off Dillingham onto narrow Robello Street. Solo pulled over, slowed and made the turn. He was just in time to see the two make another left on busy King Street, again without stopping or slowing down.

He was forced to stop at the intersection of King. The cyclists went right on Banyan Street off King, going into the Palama Settlement. Solo followed as swiftly as he could.

The beach boy whipped his cycle right on Vineyard and right again on River Street, going to Beretania.

Solo turned out onto Beretania, watching the cycle ahead through the traffic. He saw them slow down. He had figured they were attempting to shake him, but he felt now they had some destination in mind, a place where they could ditch the cycle and lose him at the same time.

The boy swung his cycle right on Aala, but was forced to straighten out, blocked by a Chinese dragon dance, loud with fireworks.

The cycle rolled uncertainly now, the boy jerking his head, looking both ways. The girl stared across her shoulder. They flicked between moving cars, forced back to King Street. Here the boy made a hard right turn into the intersection at Hotel Street and poured the petrol to it.

Solo kept after them, fighting through the afternoon traffic of downtown Honolulu until it ended at Thomas Square.

The boy turned to King Street and then left again to Kalakau Boulevard, going towards Diamond Head. He sped past Fort De Russy, now in the Waikiki beach area, passing the high rise hotels, the Royal Hawaiian, the Outrigger, going left at Kapiolani Park on Kapahulu Avenue, doubling back towards King Street.

Solo stayed in pursuit, realizing that since the beach boy and the flower girl had been forced out of Aala, they were now trying to lose him. Only the brightness of their garb and the flitting of the cycle through the cars kept him on their tail.

The boy went left again on King Street, racing towards downtown Honolulu. Solo stepped harder on the gas.

A traffic signal caught the cyclists at Nuuanu Avenue. The boy sat a moment, bracing his leg on the pavement, both he and the girl staring across their shoulders. Suddenly the boy said something to the girl and then he whipped the cycle right against the light, pedestrians leaping to safety, yelling in shock and rage.

Solo followed, seeing the gaudy-hued pair far ahead. The cycle climbed, made a turn on Pacific Heights road.

Solo was forced to slow down on the narrow, twisting street, but the beach boy saw the curves as a challenge. The road curved back to Nuuanu Avenue, and again the cycle whipped right, running scared and going inland. They went past Iolani School, the Royal museum, climbing past the Country Club golf course towards the high ranges and Nuuanu Pali Pass.

Solo glanced at his speedometer, seeing that he was doing sixty. Hillside homes and wide-spreading banyans whipped past him on the wind. On the outskirts of town he could gain on the cycle.

He stepped harder on the gas, pulling alongside the cycle. The boy and the girl stared at him for a moment, the boy's dark face pulled in a wind-smashed grimace, the girl showing only fear.

'Talk!' Solo shouted across his car towards them. The car shivered on the road. 'Only want to talk!'

The beach boy slowed the cycle. Exhaling, Solo took his foot off the accelerator, letting the car slow. When the car was down to thirty miles an hour, the boy suddenly spurted forwards on the road, going faster than ever.

Swearing, Solo stepped down on the gas.

The narrow road seemed to whirl upward through the green ranges – hairpin turns, broken-back curves. Cars headed *makai*, south towards the ocean, swerved, their horns crying out in anguished protest.

Solo pulled the car close behind the cyclist, blowing his horn at them.

The girl turned, gazing at him across her shoulder, her face set, her hair wild in the wind.

Solo shook his head, motioning her to pull the cycle over. When the boy turned, Solo waved his arm towards the roadway shoulder. The boy's face rutted into a savage laugh that refused. He shook his head, then jerked his gaze around.

It all happened at once. A car came down the road, around a curve. The boy had allowed the cycle to wander towards the middle line; now he wrenched it hard to the right as he negotiated a wide curve that brought them out on the narrow plateau of Nuuanu Pali Pass.

Solo caught his breath, seeing what had to happen, even before the cycle's front wheels struck the shale, volcanic rock on the roadway shoulder.

The cycle quivered, going out of control. The boy fought it, and the rear wheel bounced far out off the pavement. The boy pulled the cycle around hard. The front tyre struck a pothole. The cycle bounded upwards, striking against the concrete wall and going over it. Tourists in the parking area turned, screaming.

Solo slammed on his brakes. There was no sound as the cycle wheeled and skidded, going over and over down the sheer embankment towards the serene volcanic valley over a thousand feet below.

Solo let the car roll until the gas-starved engine shook, gasping. Then he stepped hard on the gas, going around the curve and down the winding road towards the far side of the island.

III

ILLYA REPLACED the pink phone gently in its cradle, cutting off the incredulous voice of the desk clerk.

He stood one more moment then, looking about this room, but not allowing his gaze to touch the corpse of the lovely spy. A breeze riffled the curtains, touched at his face. He tilted his head, seeing the sun-struck beach, the incredibly blue water and the buffalo-bulk of Diamond Head up the coast.

He shrugged the jacket up on his shoulders then and strode across the room to the corridor door. He took a deep breath, opened it and stepped out into the hallway.

'I beg your pardon.' A man's voice, cat-soft, Orientally-accented, stopped Illya.

He turned slowly, scowling because the man seemed to have materialized from the walls. A moment earlier the pink-toned hallway had appeared deserted.

For a brief moment they exchanged stares and Illya saw the shocked puzzlement revealed in the other's face – a look quickly replaced by a flat smile.

Kuryakin peered at the man's bland smile in the saffron-tinged face. Tall, with the lean rangy body one associated with a Texan slimmed down from hard work and meagre diet, pigeon-chested, knobbly shouldered, the man's narrow head had the mongrel features of a Eurasian. Thinning black hair, high forehead, bushy brows, large nose, thin-lipped mouth, his cheeks high-planned and his inscrutably black eyes tight-lidded, Oriental. He wore a brightly coloured shirt, grey slacks, hand-woven sandals and he carried a heavy cane.

Kuryakin shook his head; this wasn't an individual at all, but rather a casual assembly of mismatched parts. He turned and moved towards the elevator.

'I beg your pardon,' the man said again.

Kuryakin gestured. 'Sorry. No speak English.'

'Quite all right,' said the cat-purr voice. 'I speak six languages fluently, many dialects.'

Illya shook his head again. 'Sorry. I don't understand.'

The taut-skinned yellow face stopped smiling. 'You understand death, don't you?' Kuryakin stared at the long, glittering blade suddenly ejected from the tapered end of the cane. The man brought it up quickly and rested its needle point lightly above Illya's buckle.

Kuryakin bit his lip. 'Death I understand.'

The blade remained where it was, unwavering in the bony hand. 'I need to talk with you, sir.'

'I'm in something of a hurry.'

'Shall we talk there – in your room?'

'My room?' Illya glanced towards the closed door of the room where Ursula's body lay awaiting the arrival of hotel management and the Honolulu police. 'There's some mistake. This isn't my room.'

He saw that faint uncertainty in the man's lean face, as if Illya was not the one he'd expected to find here. The doubt was transient, quickly gone. The blade inched into the fabric of Illya's shirt.

'Inside the room, sir.'

'I don't even have the key.'

The man stared at him a moment, produced a key ring, shook one out. Still holding the blade fixed on Kuryakin, he inserted the key, unlocked the door and swung it open.

'After you, sir,' he said.

'If you must talk, couldn't we go somewhere for a drink?' Illya asked.

'Inside the room,' the man said. He touched at him with the blade.

Illya bowed and preceded the tall man into the room. They did not speak, both of them gazing fixedly at the lovely corpse.

Illya looked up, felt he glimpsed the faintest tug of satisfaction about the thin lips.

'Friend of yours?'

Illya shrugged. 'She just came in to use the phone.'

'Surely not in that condition.'

'Who are you?'

'You may call me Sam for the little while we will be in contact.'

'What do you want?'

'Must I want anything?'

'Obviously you do, Sam.'

'Perhaps I already have what I want.'

Illya nodded. 'Then you'll excuse me if I leave, since I am in a hurry.'

As he spoke he began to move towards the door. The tall man took one long step and brought up the daggerlike blade, touching its glittering point at Illya's Adam's apple.

'I insist you stay.'

'You underline your invitations so tellingly.'

Illya stepped back towards the centre of the room and the blade relaxed. Illya said, 'You mind if I smoke? – it's permitted even before a firing squad.'

Sam shrugged. 'Where do you get the impression that I am less than friendly towards you? Smoke, by all means.'

Illya shook out a cigarette, faced the tall man and flicked his lighter, wondering if he would ever get an opportunity to develop this film.

He glanced around, seeing the Scotch on a table. 'Would you like a drink?'

Sam seemed to be listening for something, but he nodded, his smile bland. 'Please.'

Illya poured Scotch over ice cubes in two glasses. He saw Sam was watching him carefully, but when he returned his lighter to his jacket pocket, he brought out a small white pill between his fingers. He passed his hand over his own glass, lifting the other and extending it towards the watchful Sam.

Sam shook his head. 'I'll let you drink this one. I'll take the other.'

Ilya frowned. 'But –'

'My dear young fellow, I don't know whom you think you're dealing with here. If you hope to outwit me, don't do it so clumsily.'

'But –'

'Oh, I know. You snapped my picture with the Japanese-made camera–cigarette lighter. I would object, but I don't think it matters – where you're going.'

'Do you mind giving me some hint as to where this might be?'

'And then you attempt to confuse me by heavy-handed legerdermain. The hand is quicker than the eye, eh? We love it that Americans and Russians oppose us in league with each other – the stupid unsubtle Americans and the heavy-handed Russians. You drop something in this glass and then permit me to see you

23

apparently doctor the glass from which *you* will drink. Not even very clever, my heavy-handed friend.'

'If you say so.'

The black eyes smiled now, in cold assurance. 'You will drink down the glass you hold out now for me. Drink it down. How do you say in the states – chug-a-lug?'

'Cheers.'

Illya held the glass of Scotch to his lips, hesitated just that fraction of an instant that would be dramatic and yet not overdone. He drank the liquid off, holding his breath.

As Illya drank, Sam smilingly took up the other glass and held it to the sunlight. Satisfied that it was free of sediment or any other contamination, he sipped at it, watching Kuryakin with ill-concealed triumph.

A heavy knock on the door stiffened both of them to alert attention.

Sam finished off the Scotch, set the glass down on the table. 'For your hospitality, thank you.'

'It was my pleasure.'

'You will wait until I am on the balcony and have closed the doors. You will then admit your guests.'

'We're eight stories up –'

'Do as I say.'

Illya shrugged and waited until the tall man crossed the room, retracting the blade of the dagger into the cane as he went. He stepped out on the balcony as the knocking grew louder and more impatient. He closed the doors and Illya saw his lean shadow through the fragile pink curtains.

He said, 'All right. I'm coming.'

The knocking was repeated, louder this time.

He opened the door, seeing across its threshold the troubled face of the hotel manager and the chilled faces of two men he supposed to be Honolulu homicide detectives.

They entered the room, and then the three of them

paused, staring down at the dead girl on the pink shag rug.

'How did this happen?' The hotel manager whispered it, sick.

'I don't know,' Illya said. 'I was not in the room.'

'Who is she?'

'I do not know. I got in the room by mistake. The wrong room. I found her here.' He hesitated, glanced towards the balcony, and added, 'There was a man with her. A tall, Oriental-looking fellow.'

One of the detectives, slender and mahogany dark, said, 'And where is this man now?'

Illya inclined his head towards the balcony. 'He went out there when he heard you knock.'

The detective jerked his head towards the balcony. His fellow, a stout man in his thirties, his temples flecked with grey, strode across the room.

'He's armed,' Illya said mildly.

The detective paused at the door, removed a snub-nosed .38 police revolver from his belt holster. He turned the knobs, threw open the doors.

The balcony was bare.

'Very amusing,' the detective said at Illya's shoulder.

'I didn't think he'd hang around out there,' Illya said.

'We are on the eighth floor,' the detective reminded him.

'That's what I told him,' Illya said.

'Oh?'

'Yes. He didn't seem unduly impressed.'

The detective did not smile. 'Neither am I,' he said.

'I was afraid that would be your attitude.'

'I better warn you. Anything you say may be used against you.'

Illya shrugged. 'I have just one thing to say.'

'Yes?'

'Have you ever had one of those days when nothing seemed to go right?'

25

IV

SOLO WALKED SLOWLY in the mid-morning heat reflected from the red-brick streets around the train station, College Park. He felt as if he were moving through an unfiltered nightmare where nothing went right and even the buildings seemed to waver rubber-like when he looked at them.

He'd been prowling for a long time. It had taken much indirect questioning to learn the names of the two young people who'd blasted over the bluff at Pali Pass.

'Polly Jade Ing,' they told him. 'She was the girl who sold leis. Kaina Tamashiro worked as beach boy at Waikiki. They planned to marry.'

Beyond this, there was little he could learn. It consumed two hours to learn that Polly Jade Ing's parents had returned to China six months earlier. She had lived over a tailor shop near the carnival park, on River Street.

Her room revealed nothing to him except that she was a casual housekeeper who wrote no letters and kept none if she received any. She had a weakness for flashily coloured spiked-heel slippers, shifts, and seemed unable to find a satisfactory hair-lacquer. A dozen different brands lined her cluttered dresser.

The Honolulu *Star* listed Kaina Tamashiro's address as only Aala Street. Solo had asked at the dozen houses, but the dark eyed people stared at him and shook their heads. Most of them did not even speak.

Solo sighed, walking in the sun. He no longer believed that either Kaina Tamashiro or the pretty Polly Jade were any more than pawns in a deadly game that had caused Ursula's death. But he had to keep pushing it now because they were the only link to whoever had hired Polly Jade to deliver the lethal lei at the airport. And Polly Jade had known there was something wrong with the deal; that was fear he had seen in her face, fear that had made her run, fear that had sent her to her death. Clearly she had been hired by a more devious employer than the Honolulu Chamber of Commerce. The lei had been deadly, and Polly Jade had known this when she had tossed it over Ursula's head – obviously she'd even known that only the upward pull on the lei would detonate it.

What else Polly had known he'd never be able to learn. But perhaps the beach boy might be involved – he had run, too, and had seemed to know why he was running. Anyhow it was a lane he had to follow all the way because he had no leads except a silver whip – and a letter of meaningless jargon.

Solo was near the shabby depot of the small-gauge railway when he first noticed the young boy. The child was the colour of beer in the sun, about nine. He wore a flowered shirt, brown shorts. He was barefooted. Each time Solo glanced over his shoulder, the boy was somewhere near him.

He glanced at the small train pulling out of the station, windows open. Across the street the military had posted 'Off Limit' signs. There were small stores, paint-peeled houses and narrow alleys.

Solo felt someone tug at his shirt.

'Mister.'

Solo was not too astonished to see it was the boy, staring up at him with round, black eyes.

'Mister, you looking for something?'

Solo nodded. 'A beach boy who's supposed to live around here.'

'I know most everyone who lives around Aala Street, Mister.'

Solo said, 'You know Kaina Tamashiro?'

'Oh.'

'Why do you say that?'

'He is dead, mister.'

'I know that. He lived around here, didn't he?'

'I know where he lived.'

Solo flipped the child a fifty cent piece, tossing it so it

27

fell into the boy's shirt pocket. The boy grinned admiringly.

'Can you take me where he lived?' Solo asked.

The boy removed the coin from his pocket, clutching it tightly in his fist. 'All right.'

He motioned Solo to follow, and ran across the street. A car wailed at him.

The boy waited at the mouth of a debris littered alley until Solo crossed the street and stepped up on the pavement, then he moved away into the narrow passageway.

Solo glanced both ways and followed.

Cats slithered between cans and barrels of refuse. Rear windows opened on the alley and voices came from those windows, along with the smells of cooking, of rancid foods.

Solo watched the boy run cat-like ahead of him. As he walked deeper into the alley a strange quietness seemed to envelop him, and to move along with him. There was tension in the silence, watchful and waiting.

A cat screeched behind him and Solo glanced over his shoulder. Two men had entered the alley behind him. One of them had stepped on a cat's tail. Solo saw that they looked young, about the age of the dead Kaina Tamashiro. They even resembled him in flesh colour and body size, as well as the casual and gaudy garb affected by the surfers and the beach boys.

He would not have been certain they were following him except that they tried to hide when he turned.

Solo exhaled heavily, looking again for the child ahead of him. The boy waited impatiently where the alley intersected with another, even less prepossessing.

'How much further, boy?'

Something in his tone diluted the last ounce of the boy's courage. The child gazed at Solo for one moment, then heeled and ran along the side alley.

Two more brightly garbed beach boys stepped from the alleyways, blocking Solo's path.

28

Behind him, Solo heard the other two running towards him.

Solo moved to the wall and put his back to it. His face set, he watched the four youthful men advance upon him.

They began to talk to him, their voices flat and cold, not waiting for him to answer, not wanting him to.

'What you doing down here?'

'You looking for Kaina, huh?'

'Kaina's not down here.'

'Not any more. Kaina's dead.'

'You know he's dead?'

'You know Polly's dead?'

'You some kind of cop?'

'He's a cop.'

'He's down here looking for Kaina. But he knows he won't find Kaina, huh? You know that? You know he's dead, huh?'

'He knows they're dead.'

'You killed Kaina, didn't you?'

'You killed him.'

They had crowded in upon him now. The two immediately in front were the only ones able to get directly at him. The others were hampered by the refuse barrels on each side of him.

It happened quickly. The two boys before him pulled out switch-blade knives, flicked out the blades.

Solo was forced to give them his entire attention. The gun in his holster seemed to press against his ribs, reminding him it was there to equalize the odds. But he did not touch it for the moment. Polly and Kaina had been mixed up in something evil, but these boys were Kaina's friends, saddened and enraged by his death, and they were boys. There had been killing enough if he could escape without it. The odds didn't make it seem likely.'

One boy on each side of Solo grabbed a refuse barrel and upset it in the alley, rolling it towards him as the two knife wielders sprang at him.

Solo saw the glint of knife blades, the gleam of teeth bared in rage, black eyes wide with hatred.

As the barrels reached him, he lunged upwards, going to his left over one and using its forward motion to propel himself hard against the first armed thug.

He heard the boy cry out and try to straighten. Solo chopped down, feeling the side of his hand contact across the boy's neck. The boy sprawled face down across the rolling barrel and Solo was free beyond him. The three remaining attackers were for the moment caught in a confusion of their own making.

As the nearest knife-carrier whipped around and sprang at Solo, Solo shook free of his jacket, snagging it by the collar as it crumpled almost to the ground.

He brought it upward, feeling the tug as the knife was thrust into it. Solo jerked the coat past him, carrying the boy with it. With his free hand Solo clipped the falling boy in the throat and at the same instant released his jacket. The boy fell gasping and writhing three feet beyond him in the alley.

The last two boys hesitated one moment, glancing at each other, their dark faces troubled. The second knifer jerked his head forwards and they leaped upon Solo at the same time, the unarmed youth striking high and the other crouching to rip upward with his switchblade.

Solo felt the fierce impact of the two stocky boys and he gave with it, going against the wall again. Another barrel was overturned; another cat howled. Otherwise the alley silence remained unbroken.

The unarmed boy tackled Solo about the shoulders, trying to pin his arms to his side. Solo could hear his heavy breathing.

Solo let the boy clutch him with both arms, still retreating. As he toppled back, he caught the youth with his fingers thrust deeply into his nostrils. He thrust upwards, hard, and the boy screamed, releasing his grip.

Still holding him helpless with his fingers in his nostrils, Solo caught his collar and slammed him down on the crouching knifer. Both of them went down, but the knifer was still scrambling forwards, and Solo felt the slicing of the knife along his trousers.

From behind him, the other boy had got to his feet, still gagging and unable to catch a full breath. He swung wildly with his knife and Solo snagged his wrist, jerking him forward off his feet. He chopped him across the neck, letting him fall into the tangle of bodies and arms and legs and alley refuse.

Solo retreated again, but the second knifer had leaped free, tackling Solo at the ankles. Solo saw the alley springing upwards towards him. As he struck, the other two boys turned and leaped upon him. Beaten across the face, Solo sagged against the wall, momentarily stunned.

They swarmed over him, taking advantage of this momentary edge. Solo saw the bright gleam of switchblades, silver in the alley light. Silver. The silver whip. Why would he be thinking about a thing like that in a moment like this? A knife sliced at his shirt, scratching at his flesh. He used his knee to checkmate that knifer and saw him fall away, heard the clatter of the knife on the ground. His extended fingers sank into the solar plexus of the next boy, pressing him downwards, relieved him of his weight, and he locked the fingers of both hands, catching them under the chin of the last one, knowing that in his rage he might decapitate him as he hurled him backwards. But he was not really thinking about the four boys, or this alley, or their knives. He was thinking about that silver whip he'd seen in Ursula's suitcase, and even as the knife point made another swipe at him, he was grinning coldly because suddenly he remembered where he had seen that silver whip before....

V

ILLYA KURYAKIN PROWLED the cell in the Honolulu jail.
Outside his cell, the detective lieutenant who had

31

arrested him sat relaxed in a cane-bottomed straight chair.

'You will make it easier on all of us to talk,' he said.

Illya sighed. 'I have told you for three hours straight, I have nothing to say.'

'You will beg to talk before I am through with you.'

'Perhaps I will. But I am not begging yet.'

'Listen.' The slender man leaned forward, speaking in a conciliatory and confidential tone. 'I am Lieutenant Yakato Guerrero. Perhaps you have heard of me.'

'I am afraid not.'

'If you had been long in Honolulu, you would have heard of me. My record as a police detective is without flaw. I did not get my promotion through any influence, only because of my record. I have no blemishes. Each case I have been assigned to, I have completed most successfully.'

'Very commendable.'

'Yes. It is. On this island, people know Lieutenant Yakato Guerrero. The law-abiding feel safer because of me. The criminal hopes I will not set myself on his trail, because I end my cases in only one way –'

'I know. Most successfully. Perhaps you will succeed with the death of that girl, but not by sitting there harassing me. You're barking up the wrong red herring. I told you. I know nothing of her death.'

'You will talk to me of it before I am through. I am a patient man and I do not anticipate you to spoil my record that has no blemish.'

'Consider me as a nothing, as an innocent bystander caught in this situation. Let me be neither a triumph nor loss to you.'

Guerrero pushed back in his chair and did not speak. For some time there was silence between them, and Illya began to see that Guerrero had not lied. The police lieutenant was a patient man, with an Oriental patience in which time hung suspended, without meaning.

Illya drew his hand across his mouth, knowing that

time was not suspended for him. Sam – the mismatched, ugly Eurasian – was incontestably a link in the Tixe Ylno matter, the affair that had seemed blown apart with the death of the beautiful defecting spy.

Finally, as if he had been continuing an unbroken dialogue, the police lieutenant said, 'Who are you?'

'I told you. I am George Yorkvitz, a bellhop at the hotel.'

'Who are you really?'

'Oh, come on now, Guerrero. You must have more to do than this! The hotel manager recognized me. I didn't even ask him. He looked at me, and told you himself that I was employed at the hotel.'

'But he could not tell us what you were doing up there. Only you can tell us this. And this is what you will tell me.'

'I told you. I was called up there.'

The dark face twisted into a pained smile. 'By the dead girl, I suppose?'

'No. I never talked to her. Someone called me. A man. Why would I call the police and report her death?'

'If you are the one who did –'

'The hotel manager himself told you that I reported the death to the desk. As an employee of the hotel, I had a right to be up there.'

The lieutenant shook his head. 'In civilian clothes?'

'I was getting ready to quit my job. I changed my clothes on the way up there.'

'Why?'

'I told you. I was getting ready to quit my job.'

'Why?'

'I came out here for a vacation. I was tired of the work. That's all. You can't make any more out of it. I don't know the dead girl. Why don't you try to find that man?'

'What man is that?'

'You could get on a person's nerves. You know that, don't you?'

33

'I never took this job to be popular.'

'I know. Only to be without a flaw.'

'I saw no man in that room with you. No trace. I found only an empty suitcase that may have belonged to the dead girl.'

'There was a man in that room. He forced me to stay there until you and the hotel manager arrived. I'm telling you the truth.'

'Perhaps you are.' The voice was low. 'If you are, you then have nothing to fear.'

'I have to fear you. You won't listen to me. You're more interested in a perfect record of solved cases than you are in the truth. How many people have you forced to confess to crimes when they weren't even guilty?'

Kuryakin had found Guerrero's Achilles heel. The youthful detective sprang up gripping the bars, his black eyes fixed on Illya's impassive face.

'Don't say such things to me! Don't ever say such things to me!'

'Then why don't you let me try to prove to you that man was in the room with me?'

Guerrero relaxed. He straightened, allowing himself a faint, superior smile. 'I think we will keep you here. We will wait for the results of your fingerprints.'

He turned and walked away, going leisurely out of the cell-block.

Illya stood unmoving at the bars, staring at the man's back. He shook his head, now deeply troubled because of what those fingerprints would reveal about him to Guerrero.

He prowled the cell. He ran his fingers through his wheat-coloured hair. It flopped back across his forehead. He knew what the results of the fingerprints inquiry would be. The FBI would send word to the Honolulu police showing not only that his name was Illya Kuryakin, but then it would have to be shown who he was and for whom he worked.

He shook his head. The assignment was already going

too badly for him to involve U.N.C.L.E. in his presence in the islands. He and Napoleon Solo had been assigned by Alexander Waverly to find a person named Tixe Ylno who might be male or female, or who might not exist at all. No one in U.N.C.L.E had ever seen Tixe Ylno – they knew only that code name which Thrush had given him. Spelled backwards Tixe Ylno was simply Exit Only – which, from the meagre clues and information gathered by agents for U.N.C.L.E., was Tixe Ylno's plan for humanity. A female spy, frightened and almost hysterical in her desire to come in from the cold, had managed to contact U.N.C.L.E. and make known her desire to defect from Thrush. Word came that the woman agent was one of the few people who actually had known, seen and talked with Tixe Ylno. She was anxious to trade her information for U.N.C.L.E.'s protection.

The frightened spy's name of course was Ursula Baynes-Neefirth.

Even the suggestion that agents for U.N.C.L.E. were remotely involved in the murder of the fleeing spy would completely destroy all chance of continuing the pursuit of Tixe Ylno. There was no doubt about it. Tixe Ylno appeared to be the most dangerous foe yet encountered by the agents for U.N.C.L.E.

He worked from the deepest network of secrecy – as attested to by the fact that not even U.N.C.L.E. knew whether Tixe Ylno was a man or a woman, an individual or a conspiracy.

Whoever or whatever Tixe Ylno was, the counter-measures had to be accomplished in a matching veil of secrecy.

Illya stared at the bars of his cell. One thought kept wheeling through his brain. He had to get out of here before there was any answer on his fingerprints which had already been flashed across ocean and continent to Washington, D.C.

He had to get out of here.

35

'You! George.'

When Illya, lost in savage concentration, did not reply to the unfamiliar name he had assumed as a hotel bellhop, the jailer scraped his nightstick along the cell bars.

'You. Yorkvitz. George!'

Illya turned from his contemplation of the barred window, staring at the jailer.

'What do you want?'

'You got company,' the jailer said. 'A friend of yours.'

Illya felt the breath exhale from him as if he had not been breathing for an incredible time. Solo must have somehow learned of his plight.

He strode across the cell. 'Yes,' he said. 'Take me to him.'

'Relax,' the jailer said. 'We'll bring him back here. He says he's a bellhop from your hotel at Waikiki.'

Illya nodded, waiting expectantly. The jailer went along the corridor to the entrance of the cell-block. The door was opened and a man came through it.

Illya stared, his heart sinking.

This was not Solo. It was no bellhop from the hotel. It was no one he had ever seen.

He shook his head. The man came towards him, smiling confidently. The jailer pointed out the cell, and leaned against the wall. 'You got three minutes, fellow.'

The man nodded and walked to the bars where Illya awaited him, puzzled and watchful.

'Hello, George.' The man was obviously Chinese, smartly dressed, his shoes shining and black. His mouth smiled, but there was no light in his eyes.

'I don't know you,' Illya said.

The mouth went on smiling; the man peered at him.

'Sure you know me, George.' His voice was louder than necessary. Illya saw he was speaking for the guard's benefit. 'We work together. Why, when I came in here, they frisked me, George.' He laughed loudly. 'How about that? Afraid I would bring you something to help

36

you escape. How about that, George?'

'How about that,' Illya said. 'I don't know you, and I don't know what you want. Get out of here.'

'Take it easy, George. I went through a lot to get in here. They took everything from me, George. Everything except this fountain pen. How about that, George?' He took the fountain pen from his shirt pocket, extending it suddenly towards Illya.

Illya stared at it, lunged backwards, crying out. In that same instant, the visitor pressed on the end of the pen and white liquid flushed out of it, striking Kuryakin in the face.

Illya tried to cry out, and could not. He tried to catch himself, but had lost all coordination. He was aware of nothing except the burn of the fluid on his skin, in his eyes and his nostrils.

He toppled back on the bed, for the moment suffocating and almost entirely paralyzed.

The man beyond the bars laughed again. 'Well, all right, George, you don't want to talk to me, I'll clear out. We wanted to help you. You don't want us to help you, that's all right, too.'

He turned, thrust his fountain pen back into his shirt pocket and strode away, complaining loudly.

Sprawled on the cot, Illya stared after him, unable to move at all. He heard the cell-block door open and close distantly, and then there was silence in the cell.

He tried to turn and could not. He lay unmoving while the FBI investigated his fingerprints and flashed back word to the Honolulu police. Illya Kuryakin. Agent for the United Network Command for Law and Enforcement.

Sure, he'd be freed then – but he might as well be dead.

He struggled, his nerve centres frantically ordering his numbed muscles to move, even to twitch, to show any sign of life at all.

He tried to cry out, and he could not even speak.

Whoever had put him here meant to see he stayed here until he was framed for a crime he had not committed, or until his true identity was established and his usefulness destroyed.

He stared furiously, frustrated and enraged, at his hands, at his feet. And he was struck fiercely again with the simplicity of the attack. First, Ursula's face was blown away by a mechanism concealed in a lei – flowers given a hundred times a day to visitors to Hawaii. Now, a visitor to the jail was carefully searched, and allowed to enter the cell-block with a lethal fountain pen – who even looked at a fountain pen in a man's shirt pocket?

VI

SOLO STRAIGHTENED up in the littered alley and put his back against the wall. Around him, the refuse barrels were overturned, a stocky beach boy folded neatly over one of them, the other three lying face down in the scattered garbage.

Solo felt a stab of pain going through him and he touched gingerly at the fire in his side. He tried to keep his face expressionless, disliking the thought of giving in to the sharp burn of abrasion and contusion marring his face. His eye was swelling, purpling, and he tasted blood in the corner of his mouth.

He experienced some small satisfaction when he looked at the four young thugs sprawled unconscious around him. The hell with them. He had not bowed to them, though his jacket was knife-ripped and stained with rancid refuse. His shirt was torn.

But he had another lead – the silver whip – despite the deaths of Ursula and the flower girl and her beach boy. He tried to smile. He had walked into a wall – and he looked it. Solo raised the back of his hand and drew it across his mouth.

After a long time, when he was sure his legs would

38

support him, he straightened from the wall and gave his opponents a sardonic bow, but carefully and not very deeply. Even so, the sky and the littered pavement changed places for a second.

He turned to walk away, but a movement caught his attention and he stopped.

The stocky boy folded across the barrel was coming around. Solo turned to him, almost sadly, caught him by the collar and forcibly lifted him on his feet, bracing him against the wall.

Solo shook him, both hands holding his bright shirt.

'Who hired you to do this?' He kept asking the question until he saw those dark eyes focus, and comprehension return to them.

The boy shook his head. Solo saw fear and admiration in the youth's face where there had once been only cold contempt. 'No. No, sir. Nobody. You see, Kaina was our friend...'

'Who did he work for?'

'With us, sir. At the beach.'

'Who else? Answer me! Who else?'

The boy shook his head, frightened. 'No. No, sir. No one.'

Solo stared at him, seeing that the boy was not lying. He was too frightened to dissemble.

Solo was calm. He held the youth's shirt, forcing him to meet his gaze.

'And this girl? Polly Jade Ing? What about her? What do you know of her?'

I have known her many years. She and Kaina. They were to marry.'

'Did you know who she worked for?'

'Only with the Chamber – that's all. I swear it, sir! Are you a cop? Some kind of cop?'

Solo sighed, deciding that the attack on him was a matter of vengeance, the need to cleanse Kaina's honour, and nothing more – unless you counted the need for violence that had spurred them.

He tightened his grip on the boy's shirt. 'I'm going to give you a chance to get out of here, away from these others. If not, I'll put you right back to sleep with them –'

'Oh, no, sir. No. That won't be needed. I should be at work already. I am much late already. There's no need.'

'Then get out of here. Move and keep moving.'

'Yes, sir. Thank you, sir.'

When the boy was gone, running through the littered alley, Solo remained where he was for another moment.

From the pocket of his jacket, he removed the sender-receiver he had used in the hotel room to summon Kuryakin. Now, after checking the alley and finding it empty and silent, he pulled out the antennae and said into the speaker:

'Bubba. Acknowledge. Acknowledge.'

He frowned, waiting. The call should have carried at least five miles. He glanced around him, thinking he wanted to clear out of here. A man could get hurt in this island paradise. Further, he wanted to communicate to Illya his need to pursue the clues offered by that silver whip.

'Bubba. Acknowledge, please.'

He spoke calmly and clearly, but without emotion. He touched at the darkening spot beside his mouth.

He pressed the button, listening.

He made one last effort. 'Bubba. Come in please. Acknowledge.'

There was no answer and he stopped listening. He reset the antennae, replaced the set in his jacket pocket and walked towards the train station in the distance, carrying the soiled, slashed coat across his shoulder.

He decided that Illya had gone off alert, because it was basic computing inside the machinery of Kuryakin's unemotional mind that if he did not hear from Solo, it was no signal to hit the panic switch. If anything he became calmer than ever, certain he was on a DC-7 winging stateside.

40

VII

SPRAWLED on the cot in his darkening cell at the
Honolulu jail, Illya looked through the bars at the
lighted corridor, at the guards and trustys moving
around out there in the onion yellow light.

He struggled violently, in a way he had never
struggled before. It had nothing to do with actual
movement, action of any kind. His body was stilled as if
in a catatonic trance. His eyes were still tear-clouded,
burning from the fluid sprayed into them. The
struggling was all inside his mind.

He began to be filled with a distracting terror that this
paralysis might be permanent. Suddenly his cell was like
a tiny box, a cheap coffin. He wondered if this were
what it all finally added up to: lying helpless in an alien
cell, among strangers. It had never occurred to him that
he would not have to pay for having served U.N.C.L.E.,
the things he had done for the united command, and the
misdoings in the years before he had joined them. He
had not looked for a reward – no more than a few hours
off once in a while to enjoy his collection of jazz. But it
was bad to know one was so alone, and helpless.

Lying there, he watched the cell-block door open and
then close. Trustys were carrying tin plates of food to
the inmates. He wondered how long it would be before
they came and found him like this. He struggled again,
ordering his hands to move. He didn't want to be found
here like this.

He heard the distant ring of a telephone. It was
silenced and he sweated, concentrating on moving his
hands.

Inside his skull he laughed when his fingers twitched,
and then bent, and then straightened. Now he
concentrated fiercely upon his feet and his legs, forcing
his conscious mind to ignore the bite of acid in his eyes
and nostrils.

His feet moved. His legs moved. He did not know

how long it was but finally he was able to sit up on the edge of the cot. His clothing was sweat damp, and he was wide-eyed and tense.

He reached out his arms, found support and pulled himself to his feet. He attempted to take a forward step, but lost his balance and sprawled outwards. He caught himself on the lavatory, and then dragged his legs after him, straightening.

He turned the tap water on full. Slowly he lowered his face into the rush of water. He let it run for a long time.

The burn lessened in his eyes, and the sting ceased in his nostrils. He kept bathing his face with the water. He realised that feeling had returned to his legs, and his hands and forearms ached with the returning strength. He bent slowly forward and immersed his face in the water.

He stayed as long as he could hold his breath like that. He heard the trusty shout at him from the bars, telling him his food was there. He managed to turn his head and nod.

He straightened up at last, massaging his face with his hands, and rubbing them briskly along his arms, trying to escape the last traces of the drug as quickly as he could.

He walked to the bars, took up the tin tray of food. He ate slowly, holding the tray, then he replaced it on the floor where it could be collected.

He went back to his bunk then and sat down on the side of it. He glanced through the bars at the corridor, then bent over and removed his right shoe.

Holding the shoe, he turned the heel and shook out a heat-bomb pellet, thinking about the force concentrated inside it. From his tray he got a spoon and scooped out a small hole under the bars. He set the pellet inside it, checking the corridor across his shoulder. He pushed a half-dozen cigarettes around the pellet, securing it. He flicked light from his cigarette lighter, setting fire to the paper.

He stepped down from the bunk then, and walked leisurely across the cell. He dropped the spoon back on the tray and leaned against the bars, trying not to watch the fire flickering in the paper around the heat-bomb pellet.

He made a mental countdown, watching the corridor. The sound the pellet would make would not be huge, but it would be enough to be heard all over the cell block.

As he waited, he tried to compute the time he would have, running across the cell, lunging upwards against those bars that would be ripped free along the bottom, but perhaps only loosened on the sides. He would have to go out that window in whatever space was blown loose by the heat-bomb. He knew it was going to be small.

At the instant the heat-bomb exploded, the wall quivering with the mild concussion, Illya heard the shouts along the cell block, the pound of shoes as men ran in the corridors.

He did not waste time to look over his shoulder. He sprang up on the bunk, shoving with his hands, finding the bars still friction-heated. He thrust outwards with all his strength, twisting as he pushed.

He breathed a small prayer of thanksgiving because three courses of bricks beneath the window had been blown loose, and his weight against them sent them falling outside the jail. Holding his breath, he pushed upwards on the bars, worming his head into the opening.

Illya's head and shoulders were outside the window. Behind him he heard the shouting of men, the ring of keys, the clang of metal. It occurred to him that surely Lieutenant Guerrero would have a special torture and inquisition set-up for captured escapees. Guerrero would never stop tormenting him if he were caught and returned now. What better admission of guilt than an escape attempt?

43

Illya pressed downwards on the bricks of the outside of the jail, thinking that he was like a woman trying to get into her girdle, only what he hoped to accomplish was to work his body through an opening too small to accommodate it.

He turned and twisted, feeling his hips sliding through, feeling the cut of the bars, the scraping of the broken wall, and feeling the pain too. The worst pain was the fear of being caught by the legs from behind, of being dragged back into that jail, squirming like a fish.

He pushed harder, feeling more bricks give, feeling his hips twist through the hole. A hard hand clutched at his ankle. Panic gave him forward thrust. He lunged outward, his hips freed. He lost his balance and went tumbling down towards the paved alleyway.

He struggled, trying to turn his body, attempting to land on his feet like a cat. He didn't make it. He struck hard, and flat, the breath blasted out of him.

Breathing painfully, Illya sat up and looked around. From above him, he heard the warning shouts of the jailers, the crack of a gun. He scrambled on all fours to the shelter of the wall, trying to buy enough time to recover his breath.

He stared down at his feet, realizing for the first time that whoever had caught at his ankle had jerked off one of his shoes.

For a moment he slumped, feeling the chill of defeat. How far could he get in one shoe? He couldn't lose himself in a crowd; he'd have eye witnesses to every move he made.

A gun fired above him and the bullet splatted in the pavement near him, galvanizing him into action, and shifting a gear in his brain. This was a vacation spot, wasn't it, a land of gaudy shirts, shorts, bikinis – and bare feet?

Trying to control his desire for frantic haste, Illya pulled off his remaining shoe and his socks and tossed them away. He rolled up his slacks above his ankles, leaped to his feet and ran along the street.

Behind him sirens whistled and alarms flared. Armed men ran from the police station into the street.

Illya pulled his shirt from his trousers, and forced himself to saunter through the gathering crowd gaping at the curbs.

A taxi driver stood beside his hack, watching the uniformed men spilling from the police headquarters.

'Cab,' Illya said, opening the rear door and stepping inside the taxi.

The driver pulled himself reluctantly from the excitement. Behind the wheel he grinned over his shoulder. 'Where to? And you ain't the guy they're looking for, are you?'

Illya shrugged. 'What do you think?'

The driver started the car, flipped down the meter flag and pulled away from the curb. He made it only to the centre of the street when he was halted by two patrolmen armed with rifles. 'Where you headed?' one of them wanted to know.

The driver shrugged, jerking his head towards the rear. 'I don't know. Got a fare here.'

Illya was lying back casually, his bare feet up on the seat. He grinned vacantly at the cops, hoping they had not seen him inside the jail. 'Waikiki, driver. Let's get away from here; I can't stand violence.'

The cops pulled their heads back from the car and waved the cab on. Illya sat up, turning, giving them a wide grin and a bye-bye wave. At the same time he was saying to the driver, 'Is this as fast as you can go?'

The driver, suddenly alerted, stiffened and stepped on the gas. He said, 'You armed, mister?'

Illya turned, his face blank. 'They so seldom arm the inmates, Charley. Just drive.'

He watched the driver's knuckles whiten on the steering wheel. When the cabbie made a sudden move to turn a corner, it was as though Illya could read the slow process of his thoughts – around the corner and back to

45

the police.

Illya leaned forward and laid the side of his hand against the cabbie's Adam's apple with only the slightest pressure. 'I think this is far enough. You stop when you make this corner.'

'Okay. Okay. I got nothing against you buddy. I just want to keep my licence.'

'I have my little ambitions, too,' Illya told him.

He stepped out of the cab while it was still rolling, and strolled through the crowd. A bus was pulling in to the curb at the far corner. He ran across the street and boarded it.

When he heard police sirens behind the bus, he touched the cord, alighted and walked swiftly down the side street. He had gone less than half a block when a Volkswagen swung around the corner ahead of him and cruised towards him. He paused, watching it, vaguely troubled without knowing why he should be. There were three men crowded into the small car – and then he recognized the driver. It was the man with the lethal fountain pen.

There was an arcade at his left; Illya stepped into it and strode along it, going past the shops that lined it towards a walled court lighted with afternoon sun. He winced, seeing the cul-de-sac, and knowing there was no chance his friends in the Volkswagen hadn't spotted him, just as they must have been watching the jail. Sam and company meant to see that he was framed for Ursula's murder, and kept incarcerated.

Near the rear of the arcade Illya paused and looked over his shoulder. The Volkswagen pulled into the curb and the three men unwound themselves from it, spreading out to search for him.

He stepped into the alcove of a curio shop. From this shadowed concealment he watched his friend of the deadly fountain pen stride towards him, his dark eyes searching the stores, watchful and alert.

Illya waited until the man passed, then he stepped

from the alcove. 'Were you looking for me, friend?'

He heard the man gasp, turning. He didn't let him get all the way around because he was too immersed in the memory and rage of what had happened to him in that jail cell. The man threw up his arm to shield himself and Illya drove his extended fingers into the unprotected armpit, and then clipped him across the neck with the side of his hand.

He didn't wait to see him fall. He moved through the astonished bystanders, ran across the curb and leapt into the unattended Volkswagen.

He burned away from the curb with the accelerator pressed to the floor. The two men ran after him, shouting, guns drawn. Over and over the wail of horns and the shouting, he heard the scream of approaching police sirens.

He roared out on King Street and kept the small car on the upper level of the speed limit, heading towards Diamond Head. When he reached Waikiki, he swung into the drive outside the pink hotel where he had posed as bellhop, where Ursula had been slain.

A beach boy sunned himself, waiting for a bus. Illya called him over. 'I promised to send this car into Vic's Garage over near Aala Street. You know the place? If you'll drive there, you got yourself a free ride downtown.'

The boy grinned, his teeth gleaming. 'Mister, you got yourself a deal.'

Illya did not even wait to see the Volkswagen driven out of the hotel parking area. He tried to move nonchalantly around to the service entrance, but inwardly he admitted he was running, even if he did manage to keep his pace to a sedate-looking stroll.

Five minutes later he came out of his room in the service quarters of the hotel wearing fresh slacks and jacket. He glanced longingly towards the cabs that would get him away from here before the police or the men from Sam overtook the Volkswagen and learned

47

from the beach-boy where he had gotten the little car.

Telling himself that nothing was ever easy, Illya went up in the service elevator to the eighth floor, where he found Ursula's room sealed by the law, with appropriate notice on the door.

He entered with a pass-key, and once inside he relaxed slightly. He laid out the developers and the small plastic cups, his receiver–sender, a binocular-loupe, a small infrared light, and the film he'd developed earlier for Solo.

Placing the binocular loupe in his left eye, he scanned the strip of developed film while the film from his own lighter-camera was being developed.

He paused, staring at the film Solo had taken of Ursula's receiving the welcoming lei from the China Doll flower girl at the airport.

He caught his breath, pleased. He could never have seen it without the jeweller's magnifying loupe, but with it he could distinguish the features of the man standing beyond the flower girl, intently watching the small ceremony.

He was not too surprised to see that it was the Eurasian who called himself Sam.

His next triumph was the excellent close-up likeness he had been able to get of Sam himself with his own lighter-camera.

Smiling, pleased with himself, he did not hurry even when he heard the scream of police sirens approaching from downtown. He sighed. If Guerrero's police were on his trail, could Sam's commandos be far behind?

He placed the pictures and the materials in his jacket pocket and crossed the room carrying the infrared flashlight.

On the balcony, he played the light along the railing top. His impassive face lighted faintly at the clear yellow stains he found there – finger marks. He knew who had left those prints. Sam had been leaving yellow-stain hand and finger marks ever since he had drunk down the

Scotch and the neuroquixonal tablet, and he would continue to put them down wherever he went for some time to come.

Illya stood there smiling, and he did not even stop smiling when he counted the four police cars racing into the drive eight floors below. He returned calmly inside the room and took up the receiver–sender, pressing its button and speaking into it, slowly, clearly, repeating himself to be certain he was understood.

PART TWO

INCIDENT AT THE HUNGRY PUSSY CAT

I

NAPOLEON SOLO STEPPED from the taxi at the corner of Third Avenue in New York City's East Forties.

He paused a moment on the curb, glancing at the large public parking garage, the row of ageing brownstones siding a modern three-storeyed white-stone. Beyond them he could see the glass and glitter of the United Nations Building near the river. He exhaled heavily, saying to himself inwardly, 'Welcome Home, Solo.' He was thinking there were moments when he hadn't been sure he would make it. But he did not smile in his small triumph because he still nursed a purpled eye and a welted, tender jaw, souvenirs from Oahu.

The street was quiet in the afternoon and Solo went along its pavement, going down the steps from the street level and entering Del Floria's cleaning and tailoring shop in the whitestone building.

The tailor, a mild, balding man in his fifties, glanced up from his work and returned Solo's faint smile of greeting.

Entering a small cubicle at the rear of the tailoring shop, Solo found himself wondering about this agent of the United Network Command for Law and Enforcement. The tailor operated certainly in a minor capacity, one of those who served mostly by only standing and waiting. He was a good tailor. Perhaps he'd once been a good field agent. Perhaps he knew nothing more than that behind his modest shop was a complex of steel, stone and bullet-proof glass housing one of the strangest and most far-flung law agencies in existence. It was unlikely that the tailor knew all the workings of U.N.C.L.E. even if he'd once been a field agent, because only a few at the top knew all its bewildering secrets of communication, eradication and prevention.

Behind the eager young faces of the men and women who entered here were the alert minds of carefully selected and wholly dedicated people of almost every race, colour and national origin.

A wall parted and Solo stepped through as it closed again silently behind him. He was in the first, outer cell of the complex; the receptionist behind the desk smiled at him as if she'd seen him only moments earlier, and placed his identification tag upon his label.

Solo winked at her and strode through the metallically lighted corridor, able to see his reflection in the deep-polished surface of the flooring.

Other agents, some in shirt sleeves, all intent, as if their minds were computers, passed him with brief glances or silent greetings. The silent corridors hummed with ceaseless activity.

Though one could not see them or hear them through the sound-proof flooring, a set of underground channels churned with the speeding launches plying in secret from moorings to the East River.

On the roofing what appeared to be a large neon-lighted advertising billboard concealed a high-powered short-wave antenna, elaborate receiving and sending gear, pulsing constantly, attuned to every change in the world around it, reaching out like prying eyes and searching feelers into every dark cranny of the world.

The battle which U.N.C.L.E. fought wasn't new; it was as old as man's conscience. Only the weapons were different now – incorporating computers, spy planes, atomic weaponry and the finest brains money could hire.

Solo wasn't a simple man, nor a naïve one. He prided himself upon his urbanity, sophistication and clear-eyed recognition of the truth about worldly matters, rather than the hypocritical things one was expected to believe and swallow. But here in this air-conditioned maze of steel corridors and sound-proofed suites, one felt the strength and the moral principles that guided it.

A door slid into the wall as Solo approached it and he entered the private sanctum of Alexander Waverly. There had been no delay and Solo knew why – every movement in these corridors was continuously monitored on closed-circuit television and electric brains scanned, rejected, or admitted one at all the knobless doors in this place.

Waverly looked up from behind his desk. The top of it was cluttered at the moment with small luminous maps, code messages and directives. Waverly's hair was toppled over his rutted forehead. His hair was black, and Solo suspected that Waverly's barber dyed it with each trimming, because if Waverly had a vanity, it was the matter of his age. He admitted, like an ageing prizefighter, to an obviously curtailed age – in his case he would tell you he was in his late fifties. No one ever disputed him, but he had a brilliant record in army intelligence that dated back almost that far. Solo supposed his superior was actually in his late sixties, but Alexander Waverly was walking proof that age was all a matter of the mind.

'Hello-uh, Solo,' Waverly said without smiling. He kept a hundred matters of utmost urgency in the forepart of his mind, but he had the poorest kind of memory for names or other trivia, even in the cases of his most highly-rated operatives.

Waverly's rhesus-monkey eyes under bushy brows seemed more vacant than ever, but Solo had long ago learned this meant the deepest sort of concentration. He respected Waverly as he did few men. It was easy to have ideals when these human heroes were at a distance, but when you worked closely with any man you got to know him well, in all his weaknesses and strengths.

'One must conclude from your report, Mr. Solo, that your triumph in Oahu was less than breathtaking,' Waverly said.

Solo smiled. As Waverly understood his agency's dangers and accomplishments, so he minimized its failures. But Solo knew how they hurt – the pain clawed at him.

'I fell flat on my face, all right. And before we go any further, I want to make a statement that I hope you won't construe as an alibi. It may well be the pattern in this case – if it turns out that there is a pattern, or even a case left after the recent setback.'

Waverly pressed a button. A wall panel slid back, revealing a small screen which instantly glowed with grey light.

'I assure you we do have a case left,' Waverly said. 'A strong case. Perhaps we are in a better position than we have been at any time previously. We must negate any past failure by concentrating on the future. Learning the identity and the goal of our friend Tixe Ylno would have been easy if we could have kept the young woman alive. But perhaps that would have been too easy. I'm sure Thrush would feel this, and this must be our attitude. Now – what is your idea of a possible pattern in this affair?'

'Simplicity,' Solo said. 'Utter simplicity. Everything so obvious that you overlook it because it's so simple.'

Waverly nodded, smiling faintly, but impressed, Solo could see that. 'Yes. Extremely clever – and sophisticated. Using simple attack in a world that has grown to look only for danger in the complex – yes. Very ingenious.'

Solo saw Waverly digesting this thought, putting it through the computer of his brain. He did not underestimate this power of his immediate superior, because Waverly was one of the five men at the peak of U.N.C.L.E.'s organizational structure. On Madison Avenue in the advertising world, it was a matter of having a key to one's private bathroom. Here it was a little more than that – Waverly was one of the few men who knew every one of the secret entrances into this building.

And it was more than status with Waverly. One reached his place of trust and responsibility only through awesome sacrifice and dedication. If any men knew every detail of the U.N.C.L.E. operations, it would be Waverly and the four other men – each of a different nationality and background – at the pinnacle of the organizational structure. The organizational chart of U.N.C.L.E. broke down the personnel into six sections, each subdivided into two departments, one of which overlapped the functions of the department below it.

Waverly, with his four associates, headed up the Policy and Operations Department. In descending order of rank, the other departments were: Operations and Enforcement – and it was in Enforcement where Solo was listed as Chief Agent – Enforcement and Intelligence, Intelligence and Communications, Communications and Security, and Security and Personnel.

It was Intelligence and Communications whom Waverly alerted now with the buzzer that prepared the screen for briefing.

A woman's soft voice rose from the waiting screen: 'Yes, Mr. Waverly.'

'The pictures transmitted here by, uh, Kuryakin, Miss, uh –' He let that part go.

'Yes, Mr. Waverly.'

'Where is Illya?' Solo asked as they awaited the first

55

briefing pictures.

'He had a bit of a sticky problem getting out of Hawaii. A matter of a murder charge.'

'Good Lord.'

'Yes. You might say that.'

Solo sank into the leather covered chair, glaring at the white screen. He bit his lip as the first picture was flashed upon it. It was the picture he had taken of the little flower girl at the moment she had tossed the lei over Ursula's head at the Honolulu International airport. It was magnified many times and showed people in the immediate background.

'This is the young woman Polly Jade Ing,' said the voice from the speakers. 'Of Chinese ancestry, she is believed to have become involved with an agent for Thrush through a dealing in uncut heroin.'

Solo sighed. One got so near, and yet fell so far short.

The picture changed and Solo sat forward. 'This man in the background is a Chinese–American named Samuel Su Yan. He was born in Dallas, Texas, attended public and private schools in Texas. He was rejected by the U.S. Army for moral reasons. He attended a university in Shanghai. For some years he worked with the Peking government as an agent in Japan, Vietnam and in South Korea. He was deported from the Phillipine Islands. He was reported killed in a plane crash two years ago.'

'Obviously he has been very much alive, working underground so cleverly that no agent of ours spotted him in all these months,' Waverly said as the picture flashed off the screen, followed by a second, a close-up of Sam Su Yan in a pink hotel suite. 'Illya Kuryakin took this picture,' Waverly said.

The woman's voice said, 'This is a closer picture of the subject, now definitely identified as Samuel Su Yan. At this moment he has been located by agents as a guest at the Acapulco-International Hotel in Mexico.

'According to Agent Kuryakin, this man accosted

Kuryakin as he left the suite of the slain Thrush agent, Ursula Baynes-Neefirth, forcing him to return to the room and to await the arrival of the police. Kuryakin reports that to his belief, Samuel Su Yan is a paid agent for Thrush. Thrush is a supra-nation, without boundaries, and an international conspiracy–'

'Come, come, Miss Uh–' Waverly said impatiently. 'Get on with it. Believe me, we know what Thrush is.'

'Yes, Mr. Waverly.' The voice continued, unruffled, as unperturbed as a delayed recording. 'Agent Kuryakin managed, by appearing to drug his own drink, to induce subject to intake ten milligrams of neuroquixonal. Neuroquixonal is a drug which causes a sweat-gland and epidermal reaction which –'

'All right! All right!' Waverly said. 'You may have time for all of the basics, but we do not. If that's all, thank you – and out.'

The briefing screen darkened and for a moment the two men sat, mulling over what they had seen and heard.

Solo said, 'Acapulco for me?'

Waverly's head came up. 'I thought your report stated you were returning here for additional information on the slain Miss – what's her name, the Thrush spy?'

'Yes. That's right. Illya and I found only a meaningless letter – and our code people confirm that it is no known code – and a silver whip. I recalled that Ursula had been part of a night-club act with another young woman in which the silver whip was a part of the important props–'

'I saw the act,' Waverly said with a faint smile. 'Well. Quite educational. Krafft-Ebbing and the Marquis de Sade could have learned.'

'I wanted to see those briefing pictures again,' Solo said. 'Until Illya turned up this bit on Samuel Sun Yan, the whip and the former partner seemed my only link with Ursula and what she became – as a spy for Thrush.'

Waverly pressed a button, gave an order, and in less

than a minute, a picture obviously some years old was flashed on the screen. The woman's voice said, 'This is the last night-club act of Ursula Baynes and her partner Candy Kane – whose real name was Esther Kappmyer. Our notes show that Miss Baynes stated she hoped to refine this act, find a new partner and return to show business.'

A small muscle worked in Solo's tautened jaw. He thought: this was Ursula's dream, her hope for a future that was now forever denied to her. She'd brought along that whip, hoping that solo and the United Network could somehow protect her from her former bosses at Thrush. She had been alive and lovely and filled with plans for a new beginning.

Solo said, 'What I need, Miss McNab, is the name and present whereabouts of Ursula Baynes' former partner Candy Kane, née Esther Kappmyer. Do you have that?'

The unseen voice from the stereo speakers said, softly, 'Of course we do, Mr. Solo.'

II

ILLYA KURYAKIN LOUNGED in the back seat of an Acapulco taxi, a vintage Dodge that limped asthmatically through the sun-struck streets, dodging the bicycles that were everywhere like fleas in the hairs of a dog. The driver batted continually at the horn, never paused at an intersection, and miraculously pulled into the curb before the Acapulco-International Hotel.

He reached back and swung the door open. 'We are arrive, *señor*.'

Illya smiled at him. 'Remind me, next time, to walk.'

'A long walk, *señor*. *Muy caliente*. In the sun – very hot.'

The resort town lay prostrate in the sun before Illya, a matter of deep browns and Mexican reds, of stout

58

Gringoes in shorts and potbellied shirts and grass sandals. The American females on the prowl and the young Mexicans stalking the streets like unsubtle beasts of prey: they'd get together, and they would deserve each other.

Illya glanced towards the blue waters below him, fair and unreal, the palms rustling like whispering castanets. Except for the people, it was a lovely place, Illya decided as he entered the hotel lobby.

The clerk told him his room was waiting for him, reserved and surely to his liking. 'Overlooking the beach.'

Illya could display no enthusiasm – he was becoming disenchanted with vacation places where death lurked on expense accounts submitted to Thrush, and yet paid in the end by the unsuspecting and the unwary.

He drew a three-by-five enlargement of the close-up he had made of Sam Su Yan in Honolulu. 'I'm looking for this man – a friend of mine,' he told the clerk. 'I was told he was registered here.'

'Ah, *si, señor,*' The clerk smiled. 'Señor Samuel Causey –'

'If you say so.'

'– In room 421. Would you like me to ring him and announce you?'

'I'd like to astonish him,' Illya said, purposely using the imprecise word.

'Of course.'

Illya turned and walked towards the barred cage of the bronzed elevator. Some transient flicker in the clerk's face suggested that he would call and announce him anyway. Obviously Sam paid well to avoid astonishments.

Sam awaited him at Room 421, standing in the doorway, a drink in his hand.

Sam gave him a brief nod and a false suggestion of a smile. 'I could have killed you as you stepped off the elevator. I'd like you to remember this.'

'You would have killed me in Oahu, if your assassins could have worked it,' Illya replied with a matching tug of smile muscles about his mouth.

'One should never assign tasks,' Sam said with a slight shrug of knobby shoulders. He wore grey slacks, a checked shirt, hand-tooled boots, looking more like a Texan than ever – one with a sense of humour that dictated a Eurasian mask. 'No matter how well-trained his minions.'

'If you want a thing done well, do it yourself,' Illya quoted. 'That's why I'm here. Would you care to compliment me on my tracking you across almost three thousand miles of ocean?'

Sam bowed, motioning Illya past him into the room, which was furnished in the Gringo decorator's notion of authentic Aztec-Mexican. Sam closed the door and turned. 'I find in you a certain native cleverness – as opposed to true intellect, of course.'

'Still, I am here, and so are you.'

'True. But I wanted you here.'

'You made this decision after your men failed to deter me in Honolulu?'

Sam nodded. 'At that moment. I was defaming you at the time for the stupid trick you engineered with the Scotch.'

Illya almost smiled. 'The neuroquixonal. Interesting, isn't it? The way it works on the sweat glands and the epidermis so the subject leaves a clear trail of yellow stains behind him wherever he goes, whatever he touches with any part of his skin. It was developed by our chemists, and its lasting power remains up to a week – and, you'll be pleased to hear, there are almost no side-effects.'

'I was pleased to leave you a trail visible to your infra-red lamps. I wanted you led to me when our hirelings were unable to stop you. I dislike having to say this so bluntly, but I mean to have you stopped. Permanently.'

'I've never suspected your intentions were any less

60

from the moment we met.' Illya shrugged. 'I only fail to see why you consider me worthy of so much of your attention.'

Sam nodded towards the portable bar. 'Pour yourself a drink. From any bottle. I assure you, my plans for you do not include the use of some chemist's trick with no side effects.'

Illya poured himself a drink. Sam strolled across the room, stood near the balcony watching him.

He said, 'In my life there have been many things I have done that I viewed myself with displeasure. I have not always approved of every action circumstances have forced upon me. Oh, but this is not true here and now – with you. I tell you. I feel invigorated and renewed at having you here like this. Your Russian smugness. Your smirk of triumph. You have outwitted three of my agents and the Honolulu police –'

'You'll surely grant me that it was a bit more than child's play – pinched between the forces of an ambitious police lieutenant and three assassins trained to kill on signal like canines? A helicopter picking me off the beach at Waikiki? Why shouldn't I be permitted some faint satisfaction of accomplishment? What does it take to impress you, Sam?'

'My father's people are old,' Sam Su Yan said. 'They lived in starvation, in oppression, in famine, flood, in every disaster known to nature and man. They learned a great patience – quite alien to your Russian stolidity. We don't look to the battles that are won, my young friend, but to the outcome of the war. Does this answer your question?'

Illya finished off his drink, replaced the glass. 'May I present my proposition to you, Sam? It may prove to be worth your while. We are quite aware of your background – even to your effects being found in a plane crash fatal to forty passengers and crew. We did not know that you had gone underground to work for Thrush. We know all about this now.'

Sam met his gaze levelly. 'For all you know, I may *be* Thrush.'

'You may be. Or you may be an underling with delusions of grandeur – some more of your ancestor-oriented viewing the end results? We are prepared to offer you our protection in exchange for certain co-operation from you.'

Sam Su Yan laughed.

His mismated oriental-Texan face worked uncertainly, pulling muscles into play that had almost atrophied from disuse. The sound burst out of him almost like a strange, off-key sob. But it was laughter.

'May Buddha look out from his celestial home to see the incredible arrogance of this puppy!' Sam laughed again, that tormented, unaccustomed sound. 'Do you truly delude yourself that I permitted you to walk into this room so that you might offer me some ridiculous cops-and-robbers trade for turning stool pigeon?'

Illya shrugged. 'I've found worse crimes in your dossier.'

'You've found nothing in my record to match what you have permitted yourself to walk into.'

Sam Su Yan's face was chilled, the unreconciled parts going hard and waxen. He dropped his glass on the carpeting and slapped his hands together.

The three men seemed to appear from the woodwork, as silent and as quick as termites.

Illya recognized one of them as the man who had attacked him with the acid-loaded fountain pen in the Honolulu jail. He supposed the other two were his fellow assassins.

He shrugged his jacket up on his slender shoulders, but made no other move.

Sam said, 'You'll forgive me if I've grown bored with this depressing exchange. When I heard you had escaped from the island, I entertained the notion that your wits might be stimulating in exchange and conflict. I know better now. You looked better from afar.'

Sam shook his head and padded about the room in his Texan boots.

He seemed to forget that Illya was in the room. He went over to the baggage rack and rummaged for a moment inside it. But when he straightened, his hands were empty.

None of the three guards moved. They continued to poise, like a kill-trained canine corps, their soulless eyes fixed on Kuryakin as if waiting for the one-word signal that meant attack and slaughter.

Suddenly Sam Su Yan gave the command. He jerked his head towards Kuryakin. 'Prepare him.'

Kuryakin spun on his heel, thrusting his hand under his jacket, snagging at the butt of his U.N.C.L.E. Special. But he could not reach it in time.

Sam's assassins sprang upon him without speaking. A hand chopped him across the neck, a hand struck him at the base of the spine, a hand caught him in the groin. Expert hands caught his arms, tore away his jacket and shirt, tossed gun and holster upon the bed.

A straight chair was pushed in behind Illya. One of the thugs said, 'Sit,' and Illya was thrust down upon the chair.

Illya struggled, and ended with his wrists and ankles secured. They worked smoothly, efficiently, deftly, and then stepped back, standing unmoving, waiting for the next command.

Illya glanced at Sam. 'Surely you have sense enough to know you can't get away with killing me – not here in this hotel.'

Sam walked towards him, his face an ugly mask, expressionless.

'I don't need you to remind me that your agents have harried me constantly since I arrived here, that they are aware you are in this hotel room. But I prefer that you permit me to make whatever decisions are necessary concerning you – because I assure you they were laid out in great detail long before you arrived here.'

63

'You'll commit a serious blunder by not releasing me at once.'

'Please!' Sam spoke sharply. 'If your men call your room in this hotel, be assured that your voice will answer the telephone. Your voice will assure them that all is proceeding smoothly.'

He walked back to the bag on the rack, drew from it a syringe and needle. He held it up to the light, forced a drop through the needle and then returned to where Illya sat watching him. 'Will you sit quietly, or must you be held? This won't hurt you as I inject it. It is in fact a discovery of *our* chemists, and I wish I could assure you it had no side effects. But' – his mouth pulled into a faint smile of pride 'I can't do that. I must tell you, as a matter of fact, that it is a matter of quite unpleasant side-effects.'

'Drugged,' Illya said in contempt. 'Carried out in the dark. What high-quality intellect devised this hoary scheme, Sam?'

'Unfortunately for you, I'm afraid you'll discover nothing hoary or old-hat in this. It's never been done quite this way – in fact this particular nerve-stimulant has never been tested on human beings, my young guinea pig. In the lab it has created some exciting results. I suggest you not be contemptuous until we learn who wins the war. Eh?' He lifted his eyes, spoke to the guards. 'Subdue him.'

Sam held the hypodermic needle in his hand, but he could not resist a final boast as the men held Illya's inner arm open to the injection.

'We are not unsubtle enough to kill you and leave your body here to draw local and international police, my friend. What we are accomplishing is much too important, and much too secret for such resulting publicity. I assure you, we have better and more long-range plans for you than this.'

As he spoke, he injected the point of the needle into the collateral radial artery from the parent trunk of the profunda brachii, inside the elbow joint. 'Slowly,' Sam said. 'This is accomplished slowly, Mr. Kuryakin. No thrust of needle and spurt of solution. This takes a little time. You will be patient, won't you, Mr. Kuryakin?'

III

THE DC-7 DRONED soothingly at thirty-seven thousand feet, with churning thunderheads like a broken wall between plane and the Californian mountains where bandits and tireless padres had marched, above the dark and choppy bay where sea wolves once hoved in from plundering to shanghai a fresh crew from the hills of the town between the bay and the ocean.

Solo smiled wryly at the thought that San Francisco hadn't changed much; the violence and the excitement was still down there in the gaudy lights and the impenetrable dark. He even remembered that during the war when his outfit had been awaiting transport to Korea, the men had been futilely warned against the gin mills of Mason Street, the friendly natives who'd insist on buying drinks. 'Don't drink with your own brother if he's been in San Francisco longer than three years – and you haven't seen him in that time.' And there was the theme song of embittered sailors: I left my wallet in San Francisco, high upon some dark and windy alley....

Solo put the thoughts of his past out of his mind. He knew San Francisco as an exciting town where pulses quickened and life took a new edge. Paris of the new world. An old cliché, but with all the truth of the tritest platitude.

He buckled his seat belt as the plane put down through the thick smoking of the clouds, gliding upon the runway.

He came off the plane with the forty other travel-mussed passengers, trying to blend in with the crowd despite his purpled eye, and the strong premonition of deadly danger ahead for him in this spirited town he loved.

He returned the stewardess' warm smile, and recalled his promise to call that number she'd printed for him on the inside of a match folder if he got five free minutes in town during the next three days.

There was a scented perfection to her specifications, and he experienced a moment of regret because he knew in advance that he would not have five minutes he could call his own for a long time.

Solo glanced over his shoulder and she waved to him from the plane exitway, and he knew with a faint sadness that he'd never see her again.

He paused at the car-rental desk and collected the keys for the Chevrolet convertible that had been reserved in his name. He saw a slender man in a grey suit lower a newspaper when he spoke his name at the desk, and straighten as the girl repeated it. The man folded his newspaper deliberately and with an unhurried stride went to the row of public phone booths and entered one, closing it behind him. He watched Solo narrowly across the administration building to the parking area.

Solo drove at fifty miles an hour in the suburban traffic on roads that sang wetly from the recent rain. The air was bracing, the flow of traffic was a challenge that alerted tired senses, and the memory of the sodden rains that struck the Bay Area stirred more old memories.

He left his keys with the doorman at the St. Francis hotel, stood a moment listening to the luring call of the evening traffic, seeing the lights and the elegantly-dressed women. He checked into the room that had been reserved for him. He prowled it a moment, anxious to be out of it and on his way as if he were a hunter with the scent of prey nagging at him.

In the street again, he rejected the idea of getting out the car. A man stalked these hills, hearing the rattle of the cable cars, seeing the streets forking out like spokes from a hub, drinking in the excitement of the strange race of inhabitants of this place. Night in San Francisco! Solo heaved a deep sigh and strode faster, going down Market Street towards the Embarcadero.

He paused on the walk, aware of people passing him on both sides, the clatter of sounds, the winking of the lights on the purple and orange neon: THE HUNGRY PUSSYCAT. *Up Three Flights.*

He walked up those three flights and entered the padded doors. The hysterical clatter of sound washed out around him.

He saw the bored faces of male and female linked like crows along the padded bar, the disenchanted bartenders moving behind it, the dark mirrors, the damp smell of liquor. Music was loud, with that muffled tone of poor acoustics. The small dance space was crowded, and here and there were military uniforms to remind one that the cold war was with him, and that this frantic city was still the port of the Pacific.

He ordered a Cutty Sark Scotch and ice at the bar and then turned with it in his hand towards the place where the largest crowd was knotted. He would have been more than mildly astonished to see that this was a goldfish pool if Heather McNab had not briefed him so thoroughly at U.N.C.L.E. headquarters less than nine hours ago....

'There she is, swimming down there. Looks like one of the goldfish, doesn't she?'

'Except the goldfish are up here and she's in a tank in the basement.'

'You've got to be joking.'

'You don't really think she's swimming around naked in there with those goldfish, do you?'

'So what's with being naked? She's no bigger than one of the goldfish,' a woman said.

'Honey, she looks better like that than a lot of us do!'

'How do they do that? Make it look like she's swimming around with the goldfish?'

'Honey, it's all done with mirrors.'

'You know that's what's wrong with life? Everything. Everything is done with mirrors.'

'Barbry Coast. That's what she calls herself. Look at her! I wonder what her real name is?'

Solo turned away from the fish pond, wondering if there would be any glamour left if they knew as he did that the nude swimmer's real name was Esther Kappmyer.

'Esther Kappmyer? Sure, that's my name, but what does that prove?' She stared at Solo from the fluffy concealment of a terry-cloth robe.

'It proves you're the one I've been looking for,' Solo said, leaning back in the only chair in her closet-sized dressing room in the building basement.

'What do you want with me?' She scrubbed at her dark, wave-rich hair with a bright red towel. He knew from his mirrored view of her that she was a thoughtfully designed young woman, and he saw that nothing improved her looks as much as being near her. And he saw something else. She was a frightened young female. Her dark violet eyes were haunted with something she never talked about, probably tried never to think about – the kind of fear that one never escaped, no matter how fast she ran or how often she changed her name.

'I never date customers, mister,' she said.

Solo gave her a smile that he hoped might reassure her. 'I'm afraid my business with you is more serious than the pleasant prospect of a date with you. Do you know a girl named Ursula Baynes?'

Her eyes widened and her body tensed beneath the robe. She swallowed hard, tilted her chin, 'What about her?'

'Ursula Baynes and Candy Kane. A dance act employing a silver whip. It played a lot of the larger clubs, and before it broke up it seemed to concentrate on the areas near sensitive military or missile centres.'

'We used to have an act together; what about it? And we used to use silver whips. It's not what we want, mister, it's what the public will buy.'

'I'm not here to censure you. I thought maybe you might be willing to talk to me about Ursula.'

She batted at her head with the heel of her hand, saying, 'I'm water-logged.' She appeared to be busy getting her body dried and warm. But Solo had seen these signs before – she was attempting to cover up how upset she was, how nervous she had become since he'd mentioned Ursula.

He said, 'She's dead. You know that, don't you?'

She nodded. 'What do you want me to tell you, Mister – what's your name? Solo? That's about as believable as mine – Barbry Coast. That has a certain nothing, don't you think?'

'How well did you know her?'

Barbry Coast tossed her head. 'Look. I don't want to talk about her. She's dead. What can it help to talk about her now?'

'You're not afraid that what happened to her – might happen to you?'

He saw her wince. He saw the way she shivered beneath that robe, but she forced a laugh. 'Why should it?'

'I don't know. Why should it have happened to her?'

'I told you I don't want to talk about it. Maybe Ursula got mixed up in something that was bad news. In her way she was a look. I don't know what it is you want to hear from me. I don't even want to know, because what happened to Ursula could happen to me.'

'Is that what you're afraid of, Barbry?'

She tried to laugh. 'Who's afraid? I always shake like this. That water's cold.'

'If you'll trust me – if you'll answer some questions the best you know, I'll protect you.'

She shivered, her violet eyes fixed on his. Her chin tilted slightly. 'You know what? Those are probably the

69

exact words you said to Ursula.'

Solo didn't speak. After a moment, Barbry said, 'I'll tell you this much. If the man who ordered Ursula's death decided to kill me, no one could protect me.'

Solo stood up. He crossed the narrow space to where the girl stood, looking small and helpless wrapped in the thick robe.

'You do know the man, don't you.'

'I don't know anything.'

'Is that why you're scared to breathe?'

'It's nothing to you.'

'That's where you're wrong, Barbry. This is a serious business. Deadly. We don't even know yet how bad it is, only that the plot is urgent enough to have involved a personal adviser to the president of this country.'

'What's that got to do with me? I'm just trying to make a buck – and stay alive.'

'A lot of other people want to stay alive, too, Barbry. Their lives may depend on what you can tell me – if you will.'

'Why do you think I know anything at all?' Her voice rose and she shook her head wildly. He saw the shadows of hysteria swirling in the depths of her violet eyes.

'You know the man who killed Ursula – who ordered her death.'

'No! I don't!'

'You know him. And you know why he wanted Ursula killed. And you've lived in terror since the moment you heard she was dead–'

'Let me alone!' Her voice lifted, shaking.

Solo caught her arms, gripping her gently and yet firmly. Her lips quivering, the hysteria building in her, she tried to break free. She could not.

She burst into tears, crying suddenly in hurting sobs. 'Oh, please let me alone.'

'I'm sorry, I can't do that. And I don't believe you want me to.'

'*You're crazy!*' She screamed it at him. 'I never saw

you before you walked in here. I never heard of you. That's the way I want it.'

'No. You don't know me. But you know – inside – that I'm trying to fight whoever it was who killed Ursula. And you know that whatever chance you have of staying alive depends on your working with me, helping me. Maybe the odds against you are bad. I tried to help Ursula. I couldn't do it. But I'll try to help you – and you know that your chances are better with me than without me.'

She shook her head, her mouth trembling, her body shaking. 'No. I'm afraid. I only want to stay alive, that's all I want. I haven't seen Ursula – not for years. That's the truth. What could I know? Don't drag me into it. Please don't.'

'Am I dragging you into it, Barbry? You knew Ursula was frightened – and I believe you know why. Ursula's death was decided a long time before she arranged to meet me in Hawaii.'

The girl sobbed openly now, almost lost in mindless hysteria. She repeated over and over, 'I'm so afraid. I'm so afraid.'

'Why, Barbry, *why?*'

'No. I don't know. Let me alone.'

Solo sighed and dropped his hands to his side. 'What if I do let you alone, Barbry, what then?'

'I'll be all right.' But she pressed her trembling hands over her face.

'No. When you walked in here and saw me in that chair, you almost fainted. Why? Because you were afraid I had come – from whom, Barbry? From the man who had killed Ursula?'

'No. I don't want to talk about it.'

'You know something else, too, Barbry. If you even suspect the identity of the man who sentenced Ursula to death, you must realize that you, too, are in the same danger that she was. You've got to have help to stay alive. I can walk out – or I can stay. That's up to you.

71

Either way, you've got to face it. Alone. Or with whatever help I'm able to give you. There's a big organization behind me, Barbry, and I can offer you whatever power they possess to help you.'

'I'm so alone. I'm so afraid.'

'You've been alone and you've been afraid ever since Ursula died. It doesn't have to be that way any more.'

Barbry straightened slightly. 'What can I do?'

Solo sighed. 'I want whatever information you have on Ursula. You won't be adding anything by telling me that she worked as a spy for Thrush. We know that. We know she was trying to break away. That's why she was killed. What we need are the people she worked with in the immediate past inside Thrush. Anything you know about them, any of them. Maybe you even know the reason why she wanted to quit the conspiracy. Whatever you tell me I promise to keep in strictest confidence. But it might be the key that will open up this whole affair.'

Barbry Coast stood immobile and stared up at him for some seconds. He saw that she was looking at him for the first time. She had been until this moment so wrapped up in the ball of fear that her life had become that she'd been incapable of turning her attention outside her own confused, terrorised mind.

Her face was rigid, pallid. She walked away from him, moving woodenly, her thoughts spinning. She appeared hardly aware of what she was doing. She went behind a screen, dropped the robe and dressed in that same abstracted way.

At last she said, 'I don't know why I trust you. Maybe like you say I've got no choice. I've got you or nobody.... Ursula trusted you, and she died ... but maybe at least she wasn't alone when it happened. Maybe the way things are with me right now that's all that matters.'

Barbry Coast sat across the white-linen covered table in a restaurant booth. She turned the daiquiri slowly in her fingers. 'You're right. I am scared. I've been out of my mind. Since Ursula was killed, it's as though I've been sitting around waiting for them – to come for me. I knew they'd find me sometime. I changed my name, my act, everything about me – and all the time I knew it wasn't any good.'

'I got to you first. You're going to be all right.'

She drew little comfort from his reassurance. She'd lived too long with her desperate terror to have it easily allayed. 'It's not much of a life being a goldfish in a San Francisco night-joint, but it's all the action they gave me, and I'm stuck with it – and I'm honest enough to tell you I'm scared to die.'

'Do you know how Ursula got mixed up with Thrush in the first place?'

She was silent for some seconds. At last she looked up. 'We were doing this act. We were free – and dating a lot. We didn't even realise that most of our dates were with military men. They were alone, had money and were looking for fun. We just got together. Then this man came along – he was a Chinese-American, a truly ugly man, though I've met a lot of ugly men who were nicer than the handsome ones. But not *him*. He told us what a high percent of our dates were with men involved in top-secret military and missile matters. He said he could get us booked only into fine clubs near these missile and military centres and that we could make more money than we'd ever dreamed of making simply by repeating to his men anything that our dates said to us. I didn't want to do it, and I told him those men never talked about secret matters. But Ursula laughed at me, and he knew better anyhow. He said all men boasted when they drank too much, especially with women.

'Ursula went for it, right from the first. She warned me that I might get in trouble unless I agreed. When this man came back for our answer, we both said we'd agree to his deal. But he said he only wanted to hire Ursula at that time. The reason – well, he said he could contact me later.

'I got ill then, seeing that Ursula had joined this man's organization. Suddenly we got a complete new set of bookings. But I was too nervous. I was getting ulcers worrying about Ursula and what was going to happen to us. We broke up the act. She went on working for them, and I tried to change my name and lose them. I was afraid – even then.

'Once Ursula and I met, accidentally, for a little while. She was thin, pale, nervous, tense, scared. She wanted out, but didn't know how to get free – and stay alive.

'We had a silly code made up of hip words, and I wrote to Ursula in our secret code begging her to make a break, to get away and turn herself in to the C.I.A., the government, anyone who could help her.'

Solo handed her the letter he had found along with the silver whip in Ursula's suitcase. 'Is this the letter?'

Barbry smiled wanly. 'Yes. That's it. It's just a jumble of zero-cool words. The only way you can understand it is to know what the other person is talking about. Ursula knew. I never heard from her again. After I wrote her, I got frightened again. I dyed my hair again, I left Chicago suddenly, and turned up out here with my new act and my new name. But I know they'll find me. They can find anybody they want to find.'

'Who is "they"? The Chinese-American that originally approached you and Ursula?'

'Yes. Him. The rest of them. But him mostly. He'll find me if he wants to.'

'Could you make it easy for him?'

'What?' She shook her head, her eyes dilating.

'I want you to let him find you. We need you to bring him out – so we can trap him.'

She shook her head. She stared at him. Her face was milk white, and her eyes empty. Her lips moved, but she did not speak. He leaped up, going around the table because she fainted suddenly, her face striking hard, straight down.

74

IV

ILLYA AWOKE and found himself lying curled upon a red and brown Mexican rug.

He shivered, opening his eyes. Remembering the injection given him by Sam Su Yan, he was astonished to find his mind was clear.

'Ah. He wakes up. Our guinea pig.' He heard Sam's voice somewhere above him.

He turned his head, but the light pained his eyes, and suddenly his whole body twitched as he had seen spastics quiver.

He tried to speak, but the words were garbled, meaningless, and his tongue felt thick in his mouth.

He heard Sam's amused chuckle, mixed with something new – a woman's contemptuous laughter. He tried to turn again, but every time he tried to move at all, his body reacted in violent and disjointed spasms.

He stared up at Sam standing like a bony vulture above him.

'Yes.' Sam was pleased. 'We are getting about the same reactions from our human guinea pig that we elicited from our other animals in the lab. Your mind is quite clear, is it?' His smile was sour. 'No sense your trying to say yes or no; it won't come out that way. The only sounds you can make are those mindless grunts of the idiot, the spastic, the victim of stroke or brain damage. Try to get up. Come on. Get up on your feet!'

Illya turned his body, aware of the tremors that went through him. When he ordered his arms to support him, his legs bent or straightened, or simply trembled while his arms flew in wild, useless motions.

Sam and the woman laughed again. She moved closer now, in a lime green shift, high heels, her hair a golden red. Illya saw her as the kind of new discovery he wouldn't want to introduce to the boys.

Sam Su Yan noticed Illya's rapt staring at the woman. He laughed. 'I'm afraid women will be of little use to you in your condition, my friend – unless you enjoy tormenting your mind by seeing what you cannot touch. This is Miss Violet Wild, Kuryakin. I'm sorry I cannot remain here any longer to enjoy the side-effects of my revenge upon you. More urgent matters demand my immediate attention. I'm sure you'll forgive me. Miss Wild will see you safely put away.'

Illya struggled frantically on the floor, managing to get to his knees before he was attacked by a sudden fit of violent trembling and sprawled out face down upon the carpeting. He lay still there watching Su Yan and Violet Wild leave the room.

He stayed face down, panting against the carpeting, his body dissociated from the messages of his mind. It was as if the drug had scrambled his nerve centres. Every order from his mind only seemed to confuse and aggravate his nerves and muscular controls.

Lying there he felt the pressure of his shoulder holster, of his gun. They were so sure of themselves they had not even bothered to disarm him.

Painfully, and after many false starts, and falls and wild muscular spasms in his legs and arms, Illya fell over on his back.

Exhausted, he lay for a moment before he attempted any other moves. Then, his forehead sweat-beaded, he ordered his right arm to reach for the gun in his holster. His left arm trembled and waved in a wild arc. But when it fell, it landed on the holster, although there seemed little sense of feeling in his fingers.

He could *see* his hand lying on the holster.

He bit his lip, sweated, afraid that his arm might suddenly fly away from the holster in another spasm. Closing his eyes tightly, he ordered his right hand to close on the holster, to cling tightly. His left hand closed on the holster, but his arm quivered all the way to his shoulder.

Afraid even to compliment himself upon his small success, Illya forced his hand to inch upward towards

76

the gun butt.

His shirt was sweat-damp, his eyes burning with perspiration by the time he forced his quivering, fatigue-aching hand to close on the gun butt.

He said the words over and over in his mind. Draw. Draw the gun. Draw.

Suddenly his left arm moved, yanking the gun from its holster. Then it swung in wide arcs, gyrating, shaking, no matter how his mind screamed at it to lie still. The fingers loosed and he watched the gun sail halfway across the room and go sliding under the bed.

He sagged back on the carpeting, too tired to care. His left arm continued to tremble.

He managed to turn his head and saw that his luggage had been brought into this room and stood with two green lightweight lady's weekenders.

He remembered Su Yan's words: 'Miss Wild will see you safely put away.'

He breathed heavily, going over in his mind the implications of this mild statement. His mind remained clear, but he made the noises of a cretin idiot and his movements were those of one who suffered from epilepsy, or a crippling stroke, or brain damage at birth. He could not even control any of his movements.

Miss Wild will see you safely put away.

Put away where?

He managed to search the room by flailing about, lifting his head only to have it fall back hard upon the floor. He was alone. They were certain he wasn't going anywhere.

He managed to hurl his right arm upward and allow it to fall across his shirt pocket and the ball-point pen clipped upon it.

Minutes later he had it closed in his fist and his shaking thumb had pressed down, releasing its point.

Holding the pen as if his life depended upon it, he rolled across the room to the small desk. Quivering, his body jerking in strange and uncoordinated spasms, he pulled himself up to his knees. He reached out and pulled the small stack of hotel stationery towards him.

The papers fluttered out around him, and he sprawled out, holding the pen in his fist.

He closed his eyes as tightly as he could after setting his shaking fist at the top left hand corner of the sheet of white paper. He gripped the pen with all his strength even though this caused the rest of his body to react in paroxysms.

He took his time. He knew he could not hope to do more than to print his given name and the word help. Even this pushed out of the balcony would be enough to alert the other U.N.C.L.E. agents in the immediate vicinity.

He exhaled at last, dropping his head upon his arm.

He cried out his success in wild laughter, recoiling from the unnatural sounds pouring across his mouth. He didn't care, it was laughter. It was triumph. It was mind over convulsive muscle.

He lifted his head, staring at the short distance to the double doors standing open to the balcony. He had only to grip the paper, roll over there and let the wind catch it. *Miss Wild will see you safely put away.*

Maybe she would, Sam.

He finally was able to force his fist to open and let the pen drop to the floor. Then he turned his attention to closing either of his hands on the paper on which he had written, *Illya. Help.*

He stared at the paper upon which he had written so agonizingly.

The sound that burst from his mouth was a sob of agony, and it sounded like one. He cried out violently, helplessly. The words his mind had struggled so long with were not words at all. There was nothing on the paper except the meaningless scribbling of a three-year-old child.

V

SOLO MOVED the spirits of ammonia under Barbry's nose.

'No.' She sat up protesting, pushing the small bottle away from her nostrils.

'You all right?'

A slight shudder coursed through her at the sound of Solo's voice. Obviously, it brought back abruptly the reason why she had fainted.

'How did I get here?' She opened her eyes, staring about her in alarm.

'There's nothing to be afraid of –'

'Let me decide that.' Her voice quavered.

'You're all right, Barbry. You fainted in the restaurant. I didn't want to attract too much attention to us, so a waiter and I walked you out to a taxi, and I brought you here.'

She met his gaze. 'Yes. You brought me here. Where am I?'

'You're all right. You're in my room at the St. Francis Hotel.'

'You're a sneaky worker, aren't you?'

Solo smiled wryly. 'Under other circumstances I'd most definitely be using all my wiles on you, Barbry. But right now I'm trying to help you, whether you believe me or not.'

'Right now I'm not so sure.'

He grinned at her. 'I had a coffee sent up. You'll feel a lot better.' He poured a cup from the glittering silver service.

She took the small china cup, sipping at it, relaxing slightly.

'Why did you bring me here, Solo?'

'What would *you* do with a woman who fainted in a public place?' He sipped at a cup of coffee. The steam rose between them. 'I promised to protect you. I can do it better when you're where I can watch you.'

'That's all off, Solo.'

He set his cup down, watching her narrowly. 'What are you talking about?'

'The agreement you and I made. I meant to keep it. But you've already broken your part of it.'

He frowned. 'Do you mind explaining that?'

'It's simple enough. I told you I was scared half out of my mind. You said that if I'd tell you what I knew of Ursula and the time she worked as a spy with Thrush, you'd try to help me stay alive.'

'And I do promise that.'

'No. You said talk. But the next thing you wanted was to use me as bait to lure a man into your trap. He's a man I'm more afraid of than I am of the devil. Talking about him is one thing. Putting myself where I *know* he can get at me – I don't want any part of that. I mean it, Solo. I'm dead afraid – and I'm not going to get involved.'

'You are involved.'

'Am I? Then I'm not going to get involved any deeper.'

He stood up. He looked down at her. 'I don't blame you for being afraid. I wouldn't think much of you if you didn't have sense enough to be scared –'

'Oh, I've got a lot of sense! I'm scared to death. Sorry, Solo, flattery won't do it, either.'

He smiled. 'All right. But maybe the truth will, and the unvarnished truth is, Barbry, you are involved. I assure you that you are. If only because you were approached by Thrush – that means they know about you. Whatever it is they plan to do now, they may be afraid to trust you. You said for some reason they turned you down, but you didn't tell me what it was.'

He saw a shadow flicker across her dark eyes. She drew a deep breath. 'I don't want to talk about it – the reason.'

'Why?'

'Because it doesn't have anything to do with this.'

He shrugged. 'That's up to you, Barbry. Everything

you tell me to help me may aid in saving your life. But what you want to tell me, and don't want to tell me, that's up to you.... But there are more reasons why you're in danger from Thrush. You wrote Ursula a letter – and even if it was in a hip jargon only the two of you would understand, it would be enough to make Thrush suspicious of you. And the very fact that you stayed with Ursula for some weeks after she started working for Thrush may mean that you – even unwittingly – met or heard from Ursula about a man that we know only by his code name – Tixe Ylno. You may have seen him, or you may know him well enough for your life to be forfeit because he'll be afraid to let you live at this critical time in his plans.'

'You know how to break a gal up, don't you?'

'It's the truth doing that, Barbry. I'm not telling you anything you haven't already told yourself these past months.'

After a moment she shook her head. 'No. I guess not.'

'And then there's the matter of this Chinese-American who approached you and Ursula in the first place. For all we know he may be Tixe Ylno. No matter who he is, he's part of this immediate business they're enmeshed in – and they don't want people like you around spoiling it for them. He loves secrecy. He even had himself declared dead in a plane crash two years ago in order to make all this easier for him. You think he's going to let a doll he was afraid to trust as a spy stay alive long enough to trip him up? I can tell you he won't. The stakes are too high.'

She shuddered, covering her face with her hands. Her body shook. Solo saw that she was numbed with fear.

'We've got to stop him, Barbry. You understand? The only way we can do that is –'

The telephone rang, breaking across his words, stopping him cold. He glanced towards the instrument, frowning.

He reached out, lifted the receiver and placed it against his ear. 'Solo speaking.'

The voice was that of a woman: the words were in the code of his department in the United Network Command. There was no doubting their authenticity or their meaning.

'Acknowledge,' he said.

'Do you understand clearly?' the voice enquired.

'Yes. Thank you.' The phone went dead in his hand.

He turned, finding Barbry Coast crouching on his bed, watching him, her eyes stark, wide.

'I must go out,' he said. 'At once. Will you wait here for me?'

Her voice was flat. 'You think they won't find me here?'

'You'll be safe here, as long as you follow my orders.'

'Safe when used as directed,' she said in a dulled tone that was devoid of hope.

'Just stay in here. Keep the door locked, the latch on. When I come back, I'll knock three times. Before you unlock the door, ask my name. Don't unlatch or unlock that door for any reason, unless you hear three knocks first and then hear my voice.'

She nodded and sank down on the bed. He glanced at her, seeing she had no hope. She wanted to trust him, but she knew too much about Thrush, and she no longer trusted anything.

VI

SOLO WALKED into *Forbidden City* just off Grant Avenue. The shops around it and the cafe itself seemed pervaded with oriental incense. One never escaped the startled little bite of shock at finding a place like this, even in a city like San Francisco. The patrons, the murals, the waitresses, the waiters, the tables and chairs seemed unreal, as if they did not even exist outside this world inside itself.

A man in Mandarin dress came forward and bowed.

82

'Ah, Mr. Solo. Good evening, Mr. Solo.'

Solo bowed, giving him a faint smile because he knew neither of them had ever encountered the other before.

'Will you be kind enough to come this way with me, Mr. Solo?'

Solo followed him through the tables towards the rear of the cafe. They went along a short, dimly lit corridor and the Chinaman rapped on the door facing.

Alexander Waverly looked up from the head of the table when Solo was ushered into the red-upholstered room. Waverly seemed entirely at ease, though Solo knew that less than five hours ago he'd been at headquarters on New York's east side, or at home in bed. Nothing ever appeared to ruffle his exterior calm. Solo supposed a man got like this when he had been down all roads, seen everything at least twice.

'Come in, Mr., uh –'

'You must know who I am,' Solo said, smiling. 'You sent for me.'

Waverly chuckled briefly and motioned him to a chair across the red-varnished table from the third man in the room. He said, 'Solo, I'm sure you know Osgood – uh, Osgood DeVry. He's a personal adviser to the president of the United States.'

Solo extended his hand. 'I'm glad to know you, Mr. DeVry. I've heard a great deal about you.'

Osgood DeVry smiled. He was a thick-set man of slightly more than medium height. There was the flushed pink, steak-fed look about him of a man who had grown accustomed to unaccustomed success and ease of life. He was in his early fifties, mildly overweight. He wore his greying brown hair parted on the side and brushed back dry from his scalp.

'Everyone who knows Osgood is proud of the work he's doing down there in Washington,' Waverly said.

'Not everyone,' DeVry said, deprecatingly, though he smiled. 'One does the best he can. Sometimes he's rewarded. Sometimes he's forced to turn the other cheek until he runs out of cheeks. I try not to think about it. I do what I think I must.'

'Yes.' Waverly cleared his throat. 'And this leads us neatly into the reason for our nocturnal call on you, Solo. It's so urgent that we had to interrupt your present mission, no matter how important, and even if it were blonde.' Waverly smiled, but there was an entire lack of sympathy in his voice.

'Perhaps I'd better fill you in on it,' Osgood DeVry said. He shifted his attaché case on the table before him. 'Though it applies to the case, some of it is personal.'

'All of it is of vital concern to the safety of this nation, and perhaps of Russia too,' Waverly said. 'And we are now certain that it concerns our friend of the code name, Tixe Ylon.'

DeVry filled a pipe with tobacco and tamped it down. He placed the curved mouthpiece between his teeth, but did not light it. Watching him, Solo saw a strong man who might have somehow weakened from the soft life in Washington. Obviously, he worked hard, but one saw that whatever he did for the president or for his country these days, it was all inestimably easier than the life he'd known in his early years.

DeVry said, 'I'm a kid who sold newspapers in Dallas streets, Mr. Solo. My folks deserted me. I grew up in foster homes. I made my own decisions – they weren't always right, of course, but I learned to stand up whether they were right or wrong. In my present position of course, I can't do anything that is contrary to the wishes of the president – nor would I want to.'

Waverly said, 'We understand.'

Solo nodded, settling back in the red, leather-covered chair. The lights from the red chimneys cast a reflected glow upon the faces of the men across from him.

'It's the matter of the decision that's important here. When I was younger – younger than you, Mr. Solo – I was a line officer in the army. I made decisions then when I couldn't get back to headquarters or there wasn't time. I can tell you, I stood or fell on them, then.' He shook his head as if brushing away a bitterly unpleasant memory. 'Well. Now what I am about to tell you, I have discussed with the president – and with Alexander Waverly here – but no one else. The president agrees with me that I must make the decision – and he has tacitly allowed me to understand that he will not be able publicly to defend me or my decision. My public life depends on success or failure –'

'We're not here to fail, Osgood,' Waverly said.

Osgood DeVry laughed, almost a desperate sound. 'No. We certainly are not. Briefly, Mr. Solo, we have come across some information that perhaps should be turned over to the joint Chiefs, Central Intelligence, the Pentagon – but it is of such a nature that even if only a whisper leaked, the entire country might panic. My decision is to deal quietly with the matter as long as we can. My decision is to let you people at U.N.C.L.E. handle it – as long as you can. Now, it's my decision, and the president concurs – as long as *he* can, and off the record. Failure will mean that my head will roll, that I will have failed the president, who's been a close friend of mine for many years – but more than that, I will have failed the people I've tried to serve all my life, whether they always appreciated it or not.'

'Failure could well mean the destruction of the civilized world,' Waverly said.

Solo straightened, staring at his chief incredulously.

Waverly smiled. 'Don't be upset, Solo. No one can hear us. This is a sound-proofed room. We could fire a cannon in here and we'd never be heard. That's why we chose this place.'

Solo sighed and relaxed. 'Then an atomic bomb is involved?'

DeVry said, 'At least, an atomic device is rumoured to be entangled in the affair. Yes. Here's what happened. One of your people, in Tokyo on a tangential matter, came across a spy for Thrush. The man was badly wounded, his stomach laid open with knife wounds. He would have no reason to lie, and your man says he was conscious and not delirious, which is what I suspected when I first heard what he'd revealed. The plan is to attack a city inside the continental United States with an atomic device – and, according to the spy, that device and the operation is almost ready. Time is running out.'

'All of this certainly reconciles with every bit of the information we gathered which puts us onto this Tixe Ylno matter in the first place,' Waverly said.

'I may as well tell you, I remain somewhat sceptical,' DeVry said. 'I cannot help but doubt the plausibility of this information, even though we naturally must run it down. We can't ignore it.'

'Not in the light of all our other facts about the activities of this Tixe Ylno,' Waverly said.

'The point that makes me most doubtful,' DeVry said, 'is the matter of an outsider striking at the United States with an atomic device. Not with our early warning system. It just isn't practical.'

'It's just nightmarish enough to be possible,' Solo said.

Waverly nodded. 'The one important matter that evolves from what we have to this moment – whether such a plot actually is in the works or not, and whether a strike could be successfully delivered against us from without or not, whether it is fact or hoax – is that we must get to this person Tixe Ylno. Whoever he is, whatever he is, he must be quickly captured, exposed, disarmed.'

DeVry exhaled. 'For all the reasons I've given you, I've reached my decision to let you people handle this – quietly, and, I pray, quickly.'

'I believe you have made a wise decision,' Waverly said. 'We have reports in our office of Thrush agents, and of apparent outsiders, enquiring of the governments of Red China, Russia, France – even the United States – for atomic components. There is afoot this secret plot to hatch some kind of atomic device that is functional. Beyond that, we have the young woman Baynes-Neefirth, who arranged through you, Osgood, for our protection. Obviously, you know that she had been in the employ of Thrush for almost a year, gathering classified information from men in sensitive roles at missile sites. Don't doubt that there is such a plot. Thrush allowed that young woman to stay alive only long enough to get to us.'

'I failed you then, Mr. DeVry,' Solo said quietly. 'I'll try not to fail you again.'

'You didn't fail, Mr. Solo.' DeVry smiled. 'Thrush had decreed that girl's death long before she came to me. Her death was one factor that convinced me there might be something to this plot of attack with an atomic device. If these people can build one, then perhaps they have the capability for a strike.'

'I don't know yet where it will lead me,' Solo said. 'But I was able to contact the young woman who was a close confidante of Ursula Baynes.'

'Good. Good,' DeVry said.

'She's been in hiding from Thrush,' Solo said. 'We were able to get to her first this time, I believe.'

'Yes, Miss Baynes told me that the young woman had completely disappeared. I was of the mind that Thrush had found her and destroyed her. I didn't say any of this to Miss Baynes, of course. I'm glad to hear the other young woman is alive and safe.'

'She's alive,' Solo said. 'Whether she's safe or not is something else.'

DeVry smiled. 'Your record is satisfactory for me, Mr. Solo. I assure you that the president himself will be most pleased when I report to him that you people are at last in contact with someone who might lead us to Tixe Ylno. Just to learn whether Tixe Ylno is male or female will be a giant step forward, eh, gentlemen?'

'JUST DON'T be impatient, my dear little Illya,' Violet Wild said in a crooning voice. She stood above him where he sprawled with the sheet of garbled writing before him. 'Were you writing Violet a love letter, you dear helpless little bug? Don't you worry. Violet will see you safely put away.'

She laughed down at him, her beauty making her heartless laughter more than cruel.

Illya raged at her, but the sounds he made were the mindless cries of a mewling child.

Violet jerked her head and a man stepped from the shadows. Illya recognized him as the man who'd first attacked him with that fluid-filled fountain pen in Honolulu.

'All right, Edgar,' Violet said. 'It is now two A.M. It is time our little Illya and I started our journey.'

Edgar nodded, but did not speak. Illya struggled against them, but his agitated movements only amused them, and they lifted him easily. Another of the team brought the suitcases. They went out into the corridor, along it to the bronzed cage of the elevator.

The lobby was almost deserted. Laughter drifted in from the cocktail lounge. A night clerk watched them disinterestedly as they half carried Illya towards the front exit. Illya cried out, but his cawing sounds only frustrated him and got no reaction from the bystanders except a glance of amused pity. They thought he was drunk, a mental defective, or both.

Violet spoke soothingly to him as they walked – not for his sake, he was aware, but for any interested onlooker.

But Illya saw that there was none.

Even the doorman held open the Kharmann Ghia door while they half lifted Illya into the split seat of the convertible. 'Has he been like this long?' he asked Violet in heavily accented English.

'All his life,' Violet replied offhandedly. It was the sort of answer one would give who has lived with a tragic affliction so long that it has lost its pain.

She went around and got in under the wheel while their bags were stacked into the small car behind them. She tipped the doorman handsomely and smiled at him. She was calm, unhurried. She tied a pale green wisp of scarf about her bright red-gold hair, knotted it under her chin. She checked her classic loveliness in the rear-view mirror and only finally got around to starting the car, putting it in gear and pulling out of the hotel entrance.

Illya glared at the speedometer. She rolled through the sleeping town at less than twenty miles an hour.

He heard her humming to herself as she drove.

He saw the flicker of headlights in the windshield, reflected from behind them.

He realized that Violet saw them, too. She glanced into her rear-view mirror, increasing her speed only slightly as they went north out of the town limits.

Illya began to feel a little better. Violet did not seem perturbed, but at the same time, they both knew the car behind them was not friendly to her.

Illya sat tensely, waiting for the moment when Violet would tromp on the gas, attempting to lose the car tailing them.

He felt a sense of satisfaction. The Mexican country was desolate, open. Losing that car would be a difficult matter on this narrow, winding road through the mountains. He cut his eyes at her, willing to give her odds that she would not make it.

She drove now at an untroubled forty miles an hour.

Illya stirred in his bucket seat.

She glanced at him. 'What's the matter, little Illya? Does my little bug think his friends will stop us?'

He forced his head around, though it jerked and trembled, seeing that the car was gaining on the Kharmann Ghia convertible.

'Look well,' Violet told him sardonically.

89

He saw at once what she meant. Another set of headlights flared behind the second car. He did not have to be told that this was Edgar and his friends. They had lain back only long enough to give the U.N.C.L.E. agents time to roll in behind Violet's small car.

'Now we shall see what we shall see,' Violet said. She laughed, showing faultless white teeth. '*Now!*'

She cried out the word and shoved her slipper hard onto the accelerator.

The small car lunged ahead on the narrow dark road. Illya felt the sharp cut of the wind. The motor hummed and the tyres screamed on the shoddy pavement. She slowed slightly when a sign warned of a sharp curve, but she was already speeding again as she rolled into it.

Her headlights raked across the grass and rock façade of the mountains. At times below them the tops of huge trees bent in the night wind. Climbing upwards, they could see the racing headlights of the other two cars on turns beneath them in the unquiet dark.

Illya was tossed helplessly in the seat. He tried to cling to something but he could not force his hands to obey his orders.

The speedometer needle wavered at eighty. They struck potholes and the small car danced, almost turning around. Violet fought the wheel, bringing them skidding to the brink of deep chasms.

'What are you afraid of, my little bug?' Violet shouted. The wind caught her words, fragmenting them. 'You want to go on living – the way you are – you call that living?'

Illya made no attempt to answer her.

He saw on a turn that Violet's car had far outdistanced the other two – perhaps for two reasons: the men in the other cars didn't take the insane chances Violet did on this unfamiliar mountain road, and the race for the moment was between those cars back there.

The third car was lunging and nipping at the one ahead of it, in a dogfight attempt to force it off the road at every hairpin curve.

'You wouldn't want them to get you away from us,' Violet shouted at him, laughing. 'Not really. Not the way you are. What do your people know of the injection you got – or even how to combat its effects?'

Illya had flopped against the side of the car, locking his chin over the door. He was able to watch the cars below them when they came out on plateaus or sharp turns.

He saw the four headlights blend until they were like one huge beam. He saw them waver and waltz crazily back and forth across the road. Once the inside pair seemed to climb a sheer mountain wall, and then fall back, levelling out only with painful slowness.

Then they came together down there again – the scream of metal was lost in the distance, but the spark and fire of metal friction was not. The cars seemed to lock, to sway back and forth from one side of the road to the other, hugged together, neither willing to back away. Each turn brought them closer to the brow of the cliff.

Violet slowed the car and he cut his eyes around, seeing a savage intentness in her face, a blood-lust in her eyes.

She seemed, with some kind of animal instinct, to sense the moment when it was going to happen. She allowed the convertible to slow almost to a crawl, her whole attention riveted on the battle between the cars below them.

It seemed to prolong itself interminably, but it was quickly over. The cars swung back and forth like one car on the narrow, twisting roadway, skirting its rim. Suddenly the wheels of the outside car peeled away the rocks and shale at the brink of an angular turn. The wheels skidded off the road. The car suddenly dropped and then went leaping outwards into the darkness. The headlights appeared turned straight up for a split second, and then they fell away and there was only darkness.

Illya heard the savagery in Violet's deep sigh, and after a moment she stepped hard on the gas.

The sun was metallic white when they lined up at the international border. Illya lay with his head on the seat rest, trying to force intelligible words from his mouth.

His attempts did not disturb Violet; in fact, they seemed to amuse her.

'My little bug just won't stop fighting, will he?' she said.

They rolled up into customs. The American officer tipped his cap and asked if they'd mind getting out of the car.

Violet smiled sadly across Illya at the young officer. 'My brother can get out, sir, and will if he must. But you'll have to help him in and out.'

Illya struggled, his mouth stretching wide as he tried to speak one intelligible word. His mind was agonizingly clear, as bright as the sunlight, but the sounds he made were those of low-grade idiocy.

'It was a birth defect,' Violet told the customs man. 'Brain damage, you know.'

'Yes. That's too bad.' He called another officer and between them they lifted Illya from the car and sat him on a chair just outside the office.

Violet stood chatting with the officers while they opened his luggage and hers, and while they inspected the passports she had. Bitterly he wondered about the one they had prepared for him. Name. Age. Cause of idiocy.

He stared at them, at the people going both ways across the border. He cried out, but it was a cawing sound and they glanced at him in shame-faced pity. No one liked to look at the mentally defective.

Breathing raggedly, Illya forced his body to bend forward at the hips until he fell off the chair. He struggled then, trying to crawl away. Couldn't these people see now that something was wrong?

They came running.

'Poor guy! He fell right off the chair!'

'Don't squirm around like that, fellow; we'll get you up. Take it easy!'

'It's all right.' Illya heard Violet's calm voice. 'He does this all the time.' She bent over him. 'You're a naughty boy.' She straightened. 'That's why we're having to put him away finally – we don't want to do it.'

They drove in silence northwards up the rugged California coast. They stopped for the night in a sleek motel on Highway 101. By now, Illya saw they'd been joined by Edgar and company. He saw that the men were still shaken by the encounter with the U.N.C.L.E. men on the Mexican highway.

He watched Violet. She was completely unconcerned about the deaths. Death had no meaning for her. He gazed at her, thinking she would enjoy torturing and tormenting the helpless. She got a strange kick from seeing him squirm and his red-faced attempts to speak.

In the morning they loaded him in the convertible once more and Violet kept the Kharmann Ghia at top speed, going north again.

In the afternoon they left the coastal highway, climbing east into the mountain ranges. They sped through a small town of stucco buildings and palm-lined parkways. They continued to climb and a chill settled through the car.

At about four o'clock Violet brought the car to a halt before the tall iron-barred gate in a six-foot fieldstone fence.

Above the gate, in fussy wrought-iron, were the words: BROADMOOR REST.

The name stirred something inside Illya's mind, troubling him, but he could not pin it down. He knew it to be a private sanitarium of some kind, created from the thousand acre estate and chateau built by a lumber and mining millionaire in the early twenties. But it was not just that it was a sanitarium. There was something more, something that had turned up with a puzzling regularity in U.N.C.L.E. briefings.

He struggled with the thought, but it eluded him. The gates parted and Violet drove through, going along the twisting lane towards the vine-matted walls of the old stone castle. He could not see the bars at those windows, but he knew they were there.

Three white-clad orderlies awaited them when Violet braked the car before the veranda. They stood on the steps that stretched thirty feet across, made of the same native stone as were the fence and the house.

The orderlies came off the wide steps and lined up beside the car. One of them glanced at Illya, then grinned at Violet. 'Is this it?'

Violet laughed and nodded. 'He's all yours.'

One of the orderlies said, 'What are you doing tonight, baby?'

Violet tossed her red-gold head. 'You'll never know, simpleton. I can't tolerate men who work for a salary. It makes peasants of them.'

She turned on her spike heels and tapped away, going up those stone steps and through the huge thick redwood door.

The orderlies reached for Illya. He struggled, fighting at them, but his arms only flailed wildly, and the noises he made were foolish, giggling sounds. He was in an agony of terror and outrage but he was unable to express anything except garbled idiocy.

VIII

SOLO PAUSED for a moment outside his room in the St. Francis Hotel. For no good reason, he felt the tightening inside that warned of danger. He shook the thought away and rapped three times, slowly. He listened for

Barbry's voice beyond the door. There was silence and Solo tensed, taking his key from his pocket.

The door was unlocked and opened as he reached for it. Solo scowled, saying, 'I thought I told you—'

He stopped speaking, staring into the blandly smiling face of Samuel Su Yan.

'Come in; we've been waiting for you,' Su Yan said.

Solo's hand moved towards the holster beneath his jacket, but stopped when he noted the small .25 calibre Spanish-made Astra pistol that Su Yan held.

'An experimental model, Solo,' Su Yan said, 'but quite deadly.'

Solo sighed and stepped inside the room. Everything looked as it had when he had walked out of it, except that now Barbry Coast sat upon the foot of his bed, staring straight ahead of her, her features rigid, her gaze transfixed; she looked like a mannequin.

'Are you all right, Barbry?' Solo walked towards her, trying to ignore the snubbed nose of the Astra that was fixed on his spine.

Barbry turned her head slowly and stared at him blankly. It was as though she had never seen him before.

'Of course she's all right,' Su Yan said from behind Solo. 'Aren't you all right, my dear?'

'I'm all right,' Barbry said in a flat, lifeless tone.

Staring at her, Solo shivered involuntarily.

'We've been looking for Esther for a long time,' Su Yan said in a conversational tone. 'I must thank you and your organization for locating her for us – and for leading us to her.'

'We have a pretty good organization for finding people who want to be lost,' Solo said. 'Even those who have themselves declared officially dead.'

'Perhaps I no longer guarded my privacy so zealously,' Su Yan said. 'You have a rich organization, underwritten as it is by so many nations with built-in missile age jitters. But it is not infallible. I proved this before – and I shall prove it again.'

'No. They're on to you, Su Yan. They've got files on you, and pictures. You're part of a regular briefing. I mention this only in case you think you can get away with murdering this girl – or both of us – and getting away with it. They have pictures tying you in with Ursula Baynes-Neefirth's death in Honolulu. One more death will bring them down on you.'

Su Yan smiled mildly. 'You fail to intimidate me, Solo. Your people know me. But my agents know you now, and your young associate Kuryakin. Perhaps the death in Honolulu attracted too much attention, just as a death here might – even one in no way involving me or my people. Besides, perhaps there is an angle you fail to consider. Perhaps we don't need your death at the moment so much as we need you stalemated – checked, stopped. Our moment is at hand, Solo. Surely you must perceive this: I no longer remain among the "dead", all our operations are accelerated, we are making moves more openly, tucking in neatly all loose ends, such as this young woman. She's not really important, merely a minor nuisance we'd rather not have running loose at this time. But in case you take some hope from this, let me tell you that your deaths – after our operation has been completed successfully – will in no way trouble us.'

Solo felt the tension all through his body, but he kept his voice unemotional. 'We all die sometime. Perhaps Barbry and I feel some reassurance in the fact that we're to be spared at all. Live one day at a time, eh, Barbry?'

The girl continued staring straight ahead of her. She did not react when Solo spoke to her.

Su Yan said, 'I'm afraid if you want to speak to Esther, you'll have to do it through me. She reacts only to my voice. Speaks only when I speak to her. Does only what I tell her.'

'Very neat hypnosis. But no better than I've seen done on night-club floors – and I don't believe you worked it through that closed, locked door.'

Su Yan shrugged. 'What you believe or disbelieve

96

doesn't interest me, Mr. Solo. I'm sure you've heard of post-hypnotic suggestion, and the fact that a subject once hypnotized can be easily put under a second, third or hundredth time – always with greater ease, if one makes maximum use of that post-hypnotic suggestion. Sometimes a word – one word.'

Solo glanced at the waxen-like face of the girl and exhaled heavily. 'You simply told her to unlock the door to you, and she did it, just like that?'

'That's correct, Solo. Just like that. As I told you. Everything is going my way now. Just like that. This girl won't look at you, or react when you speak to her; she will do anything I tell her. She would shoot you, Solo, right now, if I told her to do it.'

Solo did not bother arguing that one with him.

'Would you like me to prove that she always obeys me?' He nodded towards the Scotch and the bucket of ice on the dresser. 'Esther. Mr. Solo and I are thirsty. The three of us have a long journey ahead of us tonight. Prepare the three of us Scotch on ice.'

'Yes.'

Barbry stood up slowly and walked woodenly to the dresser.

Su Yan's voice clawed after her in its cat-like tormenting way. 'And by the way, Esther, when you speak to me, I'd like a little more respectful tone.'

'Yes, sir,' Barbry said.

Solo straightened and Su Yan heeled around, his instincts sharp, his reaction-time extraordinary. Solo relaxed. He said, 'This proves you've known Barbry for a long time.'

'Yes. I knew Esther for a while even before Ursula started to work for my organization, didn't I, Esther?'

Barbry paused, mixing drinks at the dresser. She tilted her head, facing them in the mirror, her violet eyes empty. 'Yes, sir,' she said.

She returned to mixing the drinks. Su Yan smiled, pleased. He backed a couple of steps and sat down in a chair under a reading lamp. He reached up and snapped off its light.

Barbry turned from the dresser, carrying the iced drinks in hotel drinking glasses. She extended one to Solo, gazing at him but not even seeing him.

He took the drink from her and she turned mechanically, going to where Sam Su Yan reclined with the small gun resting on his lap.

Barbry then walked away from him and leaned against the dresser as if waiting for a new command from Su Yan.

Su Yan sipped at the Scotch, staring coldly at Barbry over the top of his glass. He said, 'I saw you last at Cocoa Beach, didn't I, Esther?'

'Yes, sir.' She trembled, reacting, even in her semi-conscious state. Fear melted and ran through her body. She nodded.

'What did I tell you then, Esther?'

She didn't speak for a moment. Then she said, 'Not to try to run away again.'

'But you did, didn't you? First to Chicago, and then to San Francisco. Didn't you?'

'Yes, sir,' Her voice was like that of a terrorised child.

Solo stared at her, so fascinated by the extreme cruelty being practised upon her by San Yan that he sipped at his drink, hardly aware of its taste or the chill of the glass in his hand. Barbry had not lied: she did fear this man more than she did the devil. Her whole body was quivering with fear.

'I warned you what I'd do if you ran away, didn't I, Esther?' Su Yan persisted.

'Yes, sir.' She could barely speak. Her face was the white of chalk dust.

'I told you that I would take you back to that place you hate if you disobeyed me again, didn't I?'

The girl cried out, a guttural protesting sound. She was incoherent with fear, unable to speak even in her trance.

Enraged, Solo forgot that gun lying waiting in Su Yan's lap. Blood throbbed at his temples. His head ached, and the pressure behind his eyes was fierce. He had not known he could hate anyone as he hated this man tormenting that helpless girl – or that his emotions could make his head feel as if it were bursting. Even the objects about the room appeared wavering and insubstantial.

'What are you? Who are you, tormenting her like this?' Solo demanded.

Su Yan flicked a casual glance towards him, not bothering to tilt the gun. His thick brows lifted as if he were surprised. 'I thought you had my complete file, Solo. Your rich, far-reaching organization. I thought you knew. Do you begin to be afraid of me, Solo? Do you begin to think that perhaps I'm in another of your files? That maybe I'm Tixe Ylno?'

Solo's head throbbed. He was aware of the pounding of his pulses, the frantic beat of his heart. He shook his head, forgetting caution or reason. He lunged towards the man in the chair. 'No, I don't think you're Tixe Ylno. I think you're a –'

He stopped speaking and stopped striding forward. He shook his head, trying to clear it, but he could not. He reached out wildly for support, but there was none. He saw Su Yan make a serpentine, graceful movement up from the chair, standing beside it, watching him.

He fought to keep his balance, but the room and the world were suddenly black dark. How? The question burned in his mind, and as everything else blanked out for him, the answer came bright and clear. Under previous orders from Su Yan, Barbry had dropped a knock-out pellet into his Scotch – and Su Yan had kept him distracted while he drank it down. But in this warm darkness where he was, not even this answer mattered.

PART THREE

INTERLUDE IN BEDLAM

I

SOLO CLIMBED the long, dark, free-swinging staircase upwards from the stygian darkness of the pit. He was tired. He did not know how long he had been climbing or how far he had yet to go. Moonlight filtered through a small opening incredibly far above him, and it glittered faintly on the metal steps, and the only thought his aching brain could contain was that he must keep climbing until he somehow reached that lighted escape hatch.

He released the bamboo railing long enough to paw at the sweat on his face, at the pressure behind his eyeballs. He almost fell. He clutched out wildly, grabbing the rickety railing, clinging to it, while the round hole of light bounced like the white ball in a beer commercial.

He jerked open his collar and loosened his tie, feeling suffocated and as if he were enclosed in a debilitating heat compartment. He didn't know where he was, and he tried to think how he had got here.

He stumbled. The attempt to think only started the wild little man with his sledge hammer again banging at the backs of his eyeballs. He gave up trying to think, and concentrated on climbing. It was so far upward to that lighted round hole, and yet somehow he had to make it before he strangled in the heat, or suffocated from lack of oxygen.

He breathed through his mouth, gasping, his head tilted back and his gaze fixed on that ragged opening with the wan moonlight beyond it. It looked wonderfully cool up there in the open, if he could only make it before he fell again or drowned in his own sweat.

Solo gave an agonizing yawn, stunned with fatigue. He didn't see how he could take one more step upwards, and yet the alternative was to tumble back into the bottomless dark. He shuddered, clinging to the railing that swayed precariously. Suddenly he heard something that made his heart miss a beat. He stiffened, listening.

There was a faint whispering laugh from the light above him. A man's voice said, 'Welcome back to life, Mr. Solo. And welcome, also, to Broadmoor Rest.'

II

SOLO'S EYES jerked open. The movement almost took off his skull.

Solo turned his head, and the pain washed down through him. He saw that he was on a round, king-sized bed in a beige-tinted room with doors opening off into other rooms of a suite, uniformly decorated and painted.

There was movement behind him. He jerked his head around, instinctively tensing his body. His instincts brought him only searing pain, and a red haze that danced before his eyes like fireflies. The haze faded, cleared, and behind it he saw Samuel Su Yan. The Chinese-American, smiling faintly with that mismatched face that looked as if it had been designed by a committee, sat casually on a chair next to the bed. He had a small brown box in his lap.

Solo pressed the heels of his hands against his temples, trying to subdue the agony of his drug-hangover headache. Staring with hatred at Su Yan, he said slowly, 'If this is a rest home, it's not a very good one. I don't seem to have had a good night's sleep.'

'Broadmoor Rest is a singularly fine refuge from the world,' Su Yan said. 'Most singular indeed, as you shall discover in time. As for the pain, I'll have a nurse bring you sedation if you wish. You may well live your final hours in comfort. A man deserves peace and comfort at the end of his life.'

Solo grimaced. 'I hardly expected to hear words of compassion from you. A man who would blow a young girl's face away – with a device inside a lei of flowers.'

Su Yan's face remained expressionless for a moment. Then he shrugged. 'A mistake of Americans,' he said. 'Our allies are angels, our enemies are all soulless butchers. You would improve your relations with the rest of the world if you realised your enemies are human beings – with simply opposing ideology motivating them. We too are working for a better world, Mr. Solo – our idea of a better world. That's all. Too bad you Americans won't have time to learn this now.'

Solo's smile was cold. 'What did you do with that part of you that is one-half American?'

'What I am going to do to the rest of America, my dear Solo ... I destroyed it.'

Solo shrugged. 'Then you'll forgive me if I continue to have doubts about how genuine your compassion is. To me, Su Yan old enemy, you are a soulless butcher.'

Su Yan's face remained expressionless. 'Don't make the mistake of underestimating men, no matter how much you hate them. Do you think I want to be doing what I am? I know that a great deal of the earth's surface may be rendered unlivable for vegetation for centuries. But it so happens that I believe with all my soul that the two great powers exploit and misrule this world through the applied philosophy of might and threat.'

'Your soul?' Solo asked ironically.

'My soul,' Su Yan replied coldly. 'Yes. I admit to you,

103

I killed that young woman. I used flowers as a vehicle of death. I've killed others. I will kill again. The sacrifices are for the greater good, and I do not pretend they always make me happy or pleased with what must be done. I'd far rather be alone in my study. I am involved in a modern translation, from its original Vedic-Sanskrit, of the most ancient sacred literature of the Hindus, the Veda. There are more than one hundred extant books, in addition to the four Sanhitos, hymns, prayers, the liturgical formulae that are the foundation of the Vedic religion which dates back at least to 1100 B.C., possibly to 1500 B.C.. The Rig-Veda, hymns of the oldest religion on earth. This is what I would love to do. But this must wait – for the better day we shall bring to this world.'

Solo was sitting up on the bed now, swaying a bit as vertigo and pain battered at his senses. Be he brought himself under control and said bitterly, 'You don't convince me, Su Yan. Your pious scholasticism is just a cover for what you really feel. I don't know if you're trying to fool the rest of the world or yourself, but I do know that underneath the sophisticated scholar you're just an animal. A mindless animal with no more sense than to try to start a war that could destroy the world.'

Su Yan's eyes narrowed for an instant; Solo heard a quick breath. Then the imperturbable mask returned, and he said, 'Insult me if you wish, Solo. Perhaps it makes you feel better, like an aspirin to alleviate the pain of your failure against me. I have no objection to your being as comfortable and happy as possible. Look about you. Look at the elegance of this suite, the fine appointments. Nothing has been spared for creature comfort. You see, Mr. Solo, you may not be here very long actually, but it may seem long as the time drags past. That's why I'd like you comfortable – and occupied.'

With a faint smile, he upturned the cardboard box, spilling out Solo's U.N.C.L.E. attaché case. Its component parts had been carefully dismantled so that the cleverly rigged bag of electronic communication and survival gimmicks, as well as those of attack and demolition, were so much useless wire, plastic, copper, wool, welding, chemicals and miscellaneous metal.

Solo stared at the complete ruin, expertly accomplished.

'We turned it over to our chemists and engineers for dismantling, Solo. They were very amused by it. They found it in part ingenious, and other parts completely naïve, almost backward. As compared to *our* best efforts, of course.'

'Of course,' Solo said.

'I have returned your dismantled toys, in all their childlike splendour, to help you pass your time while you are our guest. It will help you pass the honours, and can do no harm, unless you happen to blow off your hand, or explode an eye.' He gazed at Solo. 'You will play carefully with your toys, won't you?'

'Does it please you to display your contempt, Su Yan?'

'We all have our different manners of achieving pleasure, eh?'

'If you say so.'

'Have fun, Solo. I am afraid, however, that no matter in what manner you assemble all these component parts, they will avail nothing in this place. The room is solid concrete, and completely sound proof. You'll disturb no one. But I'm sure you will enjoy trying.'

'Speaking of pleasures, Su Yan. There's one of your pleasures I'd like to enquire about.'

Su Yan shrugged. 'Ask me anything.'

'Where is Barbry? What kind of sadism are you practising on *her*?'

Su Yan gave him a baleful look of mock hurt. 'How you wrong me, Solo.'

'Where is she?'

Su Yan laughed and shrugged. 'I said I wanted you

comfortable and this would include peace of mind, would it not?' His mouth pulled in an enigmatic smile. 'I wouldn't want you fretting over little Esther Knappmyer.'

He shook a small two-inch microphone from his cuff into his palm, and spoke into it.

Barbry was brought in almost at once by a white-smocked nurse. Solo studied the girl closely. She looked tired, and there was a resigned slump to her shoulders, to her whole body. Her eyes held that empty gaze he had seen in them when he had returned to his room in the St. Francis Hotel. She remained in whatever trance it pleased Su Yan to hold her in. She was like a robot. Solo saw he would be unable to reach her consciousness either by speaking to her or touching her.

'Are you all right, Barbry?' he said with no hope that she would even look at him.

She sat on the edge of the round, king-sized bed where the nurse had led her. She stared straight ahead of her.

'Of course she's all right,' Su Yan said impatiently. 'Why shouldn't she be? She'll live in elegance here that, believe me, she was entirely unaccustomed to outside.' Su Yan glanced about the room, at the dining alcove, the impressive fireplace, the sitting room, the bath, the second bathroom. He nodded, pleased. 'Very cosy. However, I think I can give you an even happier group – by adding a member.'

His face was twisted with chilled smiling as he spoke commands a second time into the hand microphone.

Solo tensed, watching him. He stood unmoving as the suite doors were pushed open again. His eyes widened, and illness spread in the pit of his stomach, compounded of outrage and futility.

Two white-suited orderlies, bulkily-made, their faces gleaming with their sweated, almost cattle-like stupidity, their muscles thick and corded, entered. Between them walked Illya Kuryakin. His slender face was pale, his fair eyes fixed on nothingness. The difference in the way he moved, and Barbry, was that she was like a robot, mechanical, awaiting commands. Illya looked mindless, not like a robot at all, but like a zombie.

Solo stiffened, hearing Su Yan's blandly mocking voice: 'So you see, Solo, no matter how rugged things may look to you, you are *much* better off than many others, aren't you?'

III

SOLO HELD HIS breath at the sight of the two mindless bodies left with him inside this smartly furnished suite for the insane. The indirect lighting reflected itself in the flat surfaces of their eyes.

He lifted Illya's arm, tested his pulse, finding the merest trace. On the other extreme was Barbry's racing pulses, the swirling shadows in her eyes.

He looked at them, thinking they would stay seated as they were until the world ended – which might not be the too distant future unless he was able to find some way out of here, for all of them or for himself alone.

He gently pushed Barbry back on the bed, so that she at least *looked* comfortable to him. He supposed in her state, she rested as well sitting up. She lay down obediently for him, upon her back. She did not close her eyes. She lay staring through the ceiling, through the dome of the sky, through the roof of heaven. . . .

He winced, thinking that he might find a way out alone. He hated the thought of leaving them behind, and yet all he needed was the chance to get word to U.N.C.L.E. headquarters – as quickly as that, the balance would shift to their side. But if they found him gone, how long would Illya or Barbry live? If he stayed, how long would the world itself last?

Solo smiled wryly. Here he was considering the possibility of his escaping from what must be an improbable fortress.

He prowled the room, unable to sit still. Not even the complicated puzzle of the dismantled component parts from his attack and survival case could keep him at a chair. He needed *something* to make, something that would aid him somehow. There seemed a million unrelated parts spread out there, waiting, challenging. If only he knew what to do with them....

The steady hum he had noticed from the depths of this building – somewhere under him, and there were no windows that looked from this room upon anything except stone foundation, which meant this suite was below ground – the unceasing sound continued.

He found the steel bars at the windows were sunk deeply in the concrete, defying even a heat bomb. Besides, the window led nowhere. Set high in the walls were the grates of the air conditioning complex. The fireplace had once been a working one, apparently, but now it was strictly ornamental. A heavy steel plate barred the chimney opening. The doors of the room were flat-surfaced inside, with a small peep-hole, covered on the outer facing – the kind of sighting-opening in any insane asylum. The doors swung inward easily, but there seemed no way to force them open from within.

He exhaled heavily, sweated, prowling all the rooms of the suite like a caged animal, despairing, but not tired.

Lunch came. Solo abandoned his fruitless searching of the suite and sat on the linen covered table in the alcove. He ate alone. Orderlies attempted to rouse Illya and Barbry to the food, quickly dismissed the idea. As he ate, he stared at Illya and the girl, trying to think how he might lift them from this artificially imposed lethargy. The food – a roast chicken, with tiny green peas, feathery-light mashed potatoes, a tossed salad, wine and coffee – was served by a tan-suited waiter who was obsequiously polite, but watchful. The service was perfect, but the man neither asked questions nor answered them.

And then when the lunch was cleared away, Solo was left alone in the suite with the silent Illya and Barbry. He forced himself to draw a chair to the table where Su Yan had emptied the dismantled gadgets from his attaché case. Somehow he felt he was doing exactly what Su Yan wanted him to, that anything he could do would only play into his hands, or at the very best would be useless.

He refused to become enmeshed in this negative thinking. The wires, metal, batteries, plastics, all so meaningful when assembled, were like the parts of some fantastic jigsaw puzzle. He went on sitting there, refusing to permit his mind to wander from the immediate task he set for himself: he sorted all the pieces, painstakingly, with infinite patience. Perhaps if he saw what he had, he might see where he could go. Or maybe it ground down to what Su Yan had said: it passed the time.

He gazed with pride at the small stacks, piles, sets, pyramids, assortments. Plastics, wires, batteries, minute aluminium cones, empty pellets, even a communication ear-plug had been dismantled.

Solo's concentration was interrupted by the arrival of the waiter with his dinner. He was startled to look up and know that six hours at least had passed since he'd eaten his lunch. Nothing else seemed altered much. Illya remained where he was and Barbry lay unmoving on the bed. The busy hum of motors continued from deep within the earth.

'How are things in the outside world?' Solo enquired.

'It's raining, sir,' the waiter answered before he thought. Solo saw the man's face go grey, as if he were frightened because he had spoken to him.

'Don't worry; I won't tell a soul,' Solo said.

He ate the small filet mignon, drank his wine and coffee, poked at his salad, pushed the rest of it away. Alone again, he returned to his hopeless, thankless task as if his life depended on it. He was still at it when the engines ceased grumbling beneath him, when silence seeped down from the chateau above.

The congestion of parts wavered before his eyes. He yawned savagely. He got up and prowled the suite, returning to his chair. There was a tension and silence in this place now. He supposed it must be early in the morning – those black hours between midnight and false dawn. Hours when anyone in his right mind would be sleeping, he thought as he yawned again.

'And why shouldn't he sleep? – this *was* a rest home, wasn't it?'

No, not a rest home. That was just a circumlocution for insane asylum. He was in an insane asylum, so why should he assume he was in his right mind anyway?

Drowsy. He sat down in the chair and reached for a small metal spring, trying to bring his thoughts back in focus by concentrating on the parts before him. But the drowsiness continued. Broadmoor Rest, he thought. Where had he heard that name before? Something about U.N.C.L.E. briefings ... he couldn't remember.

His head nodded, and he sank forward on the table. He was asleep before his cheek settled upon the wood.

IV

HE AWOKE WITH a start.

There had been a noise behind him, and he jerked erect, turning. But it was only the waiter, bringing breakfast. He set the tray down on the table, his eyes flicking over Solo silently. Solo yawned loudly, and rubbed his eyes. The waiter started to leave, but Solo said, 'Just a minute.'

The man paused, eyeing Solo cautiously. Solo yawned again, exaggeratedly, like a man who had had far too little sleep and was having trouble waking. The waiter seemed to believe it; a faint smile touched the corners of his mouth.

'My friends,' Solo said thickly. 'They haven't eaten since God knows when. We ought to see if we can get them to swallow something. Will you give me some help feeding them?'

The man's eyes narrowed suspiciously, and Solo laughed, letting it trail off into another yawn. 'The story of my life,' he said. 'I never can get a waiter when I want one.' He sat up, running his fingers through his hair. 'Look, you've got a guard right outside the door. I'm not about to try anything funny. It's too early in the morning to get shot.'

The waiter hesitated visibly, then stepped over to the bed and looked at Barbry and Illya. Barbry was still asleep, but Illya had awakened at the sound of Solo's voice and was trying to sit up. His limbs thrashed about weakly and he sank back down.

'Looks sinister, doesn't he?' Solo said. 'Obviously dangerous.'

The waiter flushed. 'All right,' he said. 'Bring the tray. But any funny business and I'll yell my head off; remember that.'

Solo picked up the tray from the table and took it over to the bed. The waiter nodded for him to sit down with it. 'You feed him, while I hold him steady.'

Solo nodded, and the waiter approached Illya cautiously. Illya watched him coming, his eyes flickering from the waiter to Solo. Solo smiled at him, and winked. The waiter sat down next to Illya, took him by the shoulders and lifted him to a sitting position. All the time he kept his attention riveted on Solo, alert for any quick moves.

But it was Illya who exploded into action.

With wild, deadly strength his arms flailed out, striking in all directions at once. He butted with his head, jabbed with elbows, struck with half-balled fists. He had no co-ordination, no timing; he didn't look like a trained U.N.C.L.E. agent in action. But he was effective enough – the waiter fell backwards and slid off

111

the bed, dazed and hurt by several of the wild blows.

Instantly, Solo was upon him. He karate-chopped him sharply in the neck, and the waiter slumped into a heap on the floor.

Solo stood up and smiled at Illya. 'He didn't even get a chance to yell,' Solo said. 'Not that it matters – the room is soundproof, as our friend Su Yan so obligingly told us.'

A sound like grotesque laughter came from Illya's throat as he settled back down on the bed and his twitching arms and legs relaxed. Solo's eyes narrowed for a moment. The sight of Illya in this state cut deeply into him. But he'd have to leave him here; there would be no chance of escape if he tried to take him along.

Quickly, Solo stripped the waiter and changed clothes with him. They were nearly of a size, fortunately, so the waiter's uniform fitted Solo reasonably well. Stepping to the door, he knocked on it in the pattern he had noted the waiter use last time he had been there. After a moment there was a buzzing as the lock was electronically freed.

Solo stepped through, his head down as if in thought. The guard glanced at him, and then took another look. Solo could almost see the guard adding it up in his mind and getting the wrong answer every time. But the few seconds' delay caused by Solo's having the uniform on was enough. The guard lunged for the warning button, but Solo struck him at the nape of the neck, caught him, heeled him around and shoved him through the door into his suite.

The door swung shut, and Solo looked around him. At this hour the subterranean corridor was silent and empty, deeply shadowed. At its end was a bank of elevators; Solo strode towards them. He stepped inside one that stood open with garbage cans lined outside it – apparently a maintenance elevator. They weren't likely to be watching this one as closely as the others. He pressed the button marked 'I'.

When the elevator bumped to a stop and the doors opened at ground level Solo stepped out, walking purposefully. He turned left, because that was as good a way to turn as any, and a little way down the hall he saw a red lettered exit sign marked *Maintenance*.

He strode to it, then paused, looking for a handle or button to open it. There was none. He felt a twist of panic. If anyone should see him standing there searching the panels beside the door it would be obvious that he wasn't a waiter, despite his uniform.

He reached out and ran his fingers quickly along the door jamb, trying to control his mounting tension. His finger brushed an inset plastic bar. It gave slightly under his touch. Exhaling, he pressed it harder, hearing the door-lock buzz. He shoved the door, pushing it open, feeling the chill of early morning air sweep in across his face.

He stepped through the door, almost afraid to glance over his shoulder. Never look back. Keep your eye on the future.

The door sighed closed behind him, making a flat brick wall of the rear of the huge chalet. He found himself in a grease-tanned cement courtyard with dozens of metal refuse containers lined like soldiers at attention.

The morning was far from silent out here. There was a discordant symphony of sounds: the disturbed barking of police dogs beyond the fifteen-car stone garage, the pulsing of generators, the keen wind out of the high mountains rustling the eucalyptus trees.

He walked towards the front of the courtyard, off the cement and onto the firm, well-tended grounds surrounding Broadmoor Rest. There were guards stationed in strategic places all over the grounds; several of them glanced up as he stepped out into the open. But their glances bounced off his uniform and back to the silent boredom of their sentry duty.

The morning was still only dimly lit by the sun peeping over the mountains in the east. Wind flung the manes of the trees wildly. And the dogs kept barking. Did they always bark? Solo wondered as he kept going purposefully across the grounds, neither too fast nor too slow.

Suddenly the barking of the dogs became a roaring cacophony.

As if that were an electronic impulse setting them off, white lights abruptly hissed on all over the grounds, turning the lawn into a brilliantly illumined cage set down in the dark morning. A rifle fired, the bullet humming only feet above Solo. The barking dogs raced from the kennels. Men came running from all directions.

Solo whirled, looking for cover. But there was none out here; he was all alone on the flat expanse of the grounds, without even a bush to duck behind.

And then he was not alone at all. The guards surrounded him, guns held at the ready. Canine-trainers fought the huge dogs slathering at their leashes.

And something crashed into the back of his head, sending him sprawling to his knees. He saw the grass fresh and dew-covered before him, then another blow drove everything into blackness.

V

THE HEAD SECURITY guard's voice snapped out. The two men who had clubbed Solo into the ground now stepped back reluctantly and stood at attention. The security officer spoke in denunciatory tone:

'The orders were to stop him, not to kill him or to beat him. Which one of you wants to be responsible for a dead body on your hands now when the leader gets here? Would you like to explain it, Warner? You, Merric?'

One of the guards found the temerity to speak in reply: 'We only wanted to be sure he would know what to expect if he tried it again, sir.'

While they spoke above him, Solo lay flat, staring in a puzzled way at the lighted field.

The lights were set in banks on a space three to five times the length of a football field. The grass was close clipped, the ground hard-packed. Enough for what? Nobody needed this kind of light to illumine a park in order to run down inmates on the loose.

Four guards carried Solo slowly back into the building and down the elevator, returning him to his room. He read the time on the wrist watch of one of them. It was after six in the morning. His smile was wry. He had no idea what day. Doomsday, perhaps?

They tossed him into the suite like a sack of cheap coffee, and walked out. The door slid closed without a whisper.

Solo lay on the floor for a moment, unable to get two thoughts out of his mind. The first was the size and shape of that lighted area out there. The answer struck him suddenly with the fierce impact of a thunderclap. An air strip. It was a long plateau, flat and level on the hip of a mountain larger than Rhode Island. An air strip where even a fan jet could set down.

He sat up suddenly, thinking about that lighted air strip and what the security officer had shouted at his men: *Which one of you wants to be responsible for a dead body on your hands now when the leader gets here?*

Solo got to his feet, the pain of the battering he'd taken on the field forgotten, his mind racing. The leader arriving? This had to be Tixe Ylno. And this meant his hunch had been right – Su Yan was a big wheel, but he wasn't Tixe Ylno. He hadn't dared to kill him and Barbry and leave their bodies in San Francisco. Su Yan was acting on orders, too.

Su Yan had boasted in that hotel room that everything was in readiness. The dying spy in Tokyo had revealed an awesome plot involving an atomic device.

Solo breathed out heavily. Perhaps it *was* doomsday,

115

after all. Six A.M. the morning of doomsday.

He prowled the room, listening for the sound of an arriving plane, but knowing he could not hear it. These underground walls were sound proofed.

He stared hopelessly at Illya. When he spoke to him, it seemed to him once that Kuryakin shook his head, but he could not get him to repeat it. There was a razor-sharp mind behind those eyes, but it was trapped, held incommunicado in a useless body.

Solo went to the table where the countless component parts of his attack gadgetry were sorted out. He glanced across his shoulders at Illya, then back at the wires, the batteries.

He sat down, gathering the batteries, wires, building a simple ground and a metal contact. He set the contraption on a sideboard. Getting a damp cloth from the bathroom, he soaked Illya's hands and arms and then led him to the sideboard.

He placed Illya's hands on the metal contact pieces, made the connection between the positive and negative wires. Illya flinched, leaping back. He made a small whimpering sound, but then merely stood, staring, eyes empty.

'Come on, Illya,' Solo said. 'It's got to work.'

He pushed Kuryakin's hands against the contacts a second time. Illya cried out, and his limbs jerked spasmodically for long seconds. Then he lay still, staring hopelessly at Solo. It was no use; whatever Su Yan had done to Illya could not be broken through by electric shock. Solo sighed, and returned Illya to the bed.

He shook Barbry. She opened her eyes, followed him blankly to the setup on the sideboard.

He closed her dampened hands on the contacts, crossed the wires and Barbry cried out, lunging away from it.

He caught her in his arms, watching her face. He saw the slow return of colour, the way her eyes focused as though she were awakening from a deep sleep.

She straightened, looking about the beige-toned suite. She did not appear particularly astonished to be in this place.

'I was in your room – at the hotel,' she said. 'And Sam Su Yan came to the door.' When Solo nodded, she continued matter of factly: 'I know this place. Broadmoor Rest. I was – here once before.'

Solo didn't speak, watching her. Barbry drew a deep breath. 'I had a nervous breakdown – they sent me here. I saw Su Yan here for the first time.... I didn't want to tell you before, but that was the real reason why Su Yan refused to hire me to spy for Thrush when he hired Ursula. He knew I'd had a breakdown; he was afraid I'd break under tension. That's why they tried to watch me – they were afraid to trust me with the little I knew.'

'What do you know about this place? Is it really a private sanitarium, or something else?'

She frowned. 'It was a sanitarium once, yes. But then Su Yan got control of it, and it's changed. I'm not sure....'

'What was this threat Su Yan held over you?'

She sighed. 'I knew that Ursula worked for him – for Thrush. he told me if I ever breathed a word about it to anyone, he'd see that I was committed to this place for life. It looks like he's done it.'

Solo did not say anything, because he saw no reason for holding out empty hopes for her. Her nerves were fragile enough without being strained with the awesome facts of life in this place.

He was pleased when, frightened, she succumbed to a natural fatigue and sank down on the bed, soon deeply asleep.

He heard the inner hum of motors from the earth beneath him. Stacking chair upon table, he pressed his ear to the air conditioning duct grate, but the sounds through the building were like vague, confused whispers, always subordinated to the throb of the unexplained engines.

He jumped down from the chair, replaced it as it had been. It occurred to him that listening devices were one of the easiest gimmicks to assemble. He strode to his table of sorted parts. Using the small aluminium cones, he fashioned larger ones from all available aluminium which he then formed into a telescopic rod. With an amplifier from the dismantled sender-listening set, and the reassembled ear-plugs, he had himself a directional sound pickup.

Returning to the duct-grate, he aimed the cones, inserted the ear-plug which was connected to the sound amplifier.

He smiled in cold pleasure. While the sounds he was able to pick up through the elaborate air conditioning system were faint, he could by moving the cones locate the direction of each different sound.

He examined the duct-grate closely, but finally had to give up the idea of getting out that way. The grate was very solidly welded into the wall – a first-class piece of modern workmanship.

But that thought gave him a different idea. The air conditioning had been added to Broadmoor Rest comparatively recently, but the building itself was an old one, probably dating back to the last century. A staid, respectable site for a Thrush retreat ... but perhaps with a few chinks in the armour.

Solo strode to the fireplace in the corner, knelt and looked again at the heavy metal plate which blocked off the chimney. He smiled slightly. It was as he'd hoped: the chimney itself was constructed of bricks, so it had been impossible to secure the plate any more firmly than by the use of bolts. And bolts, unlike welding, could be removed comparatively easily.

It took him less than half an hour to get the metal plate out of the way. By the time he finished he was covered with soot that had probably been there for fifty years or more – since whenever the old mansion had been turned into an exclusive private sanitarium, and this room into isolation quarters. Looking into the chimney, he found that it led both downwards and upwards. Apparently the level he was on wasn't yet the lowest one at Broadmoor; he'd suspected that, from his use of the directional sound pickup at the air conditioning grate. There had been the muffled sound of engines somewhere below.

He took one last look around the room, at Illya and Barbry, both asleep. Then he shoved the sound-directional detector into the chimney ahead of him and worked his way into it.

Bracing feet and shoulders against the rough walls of the chimney, he inched his way downwards into darkness. Loosened soot and dirt cascaded around him; he had to move doubly carefully to avoid stirring so much of it that he'd be unable to breathe. Twice he gulped in lungfuls of mostly soot, and barely managed to keep from breaking out into coughing fits. Then the soot would sink into the darkness beneath him and he would breathe in tortured gasps of comparatively clean air.

The passage was apparently the main chimney for this part of the building; Solo passed several branches which apparently led to other sealed-off fireplaces. At one point light entered the shaft, and as Solo reached the place he saw another branch leading to another fireplace, this one not sealed off. No sound came from the room; apparently it was unused. From what he could see from the passageway it seemed to be just a storeroom. He went on, still downwards towards the machine-sounds, which were growing steadily louder.

At last he reached the bottom. The sounds had by now become a deep drumming which filled the shaft with almost physical waves of sound. There was light here, bright light – another unsealed opening. Solo approached it cautiously, as silently as possible even though he knew any sound he made would almost certainly be lost amid the engine-noise below.

Then his feet touched a bed of soft ashes, and he sank into them nearly up to his knees. There was a semi-brittle crust to the ashpile, as though it had lain undisturbed for scores of years. Except for where his feet sank into them, the ashes remained undisturbed.

It was a large burning area, Solo saw – apparently it had been used originally as the main incinerator for the building. Now, with the ashes settled to a depth of only a few feet, the unused incinerator formed a small, shadowed room with an opening about three feet square through which brilliant white light lanced sharply. Solo paused, then knelt slowly, letting his eyes grow accustomed to the light before he risked a look outside.

When he did, he stared out into a hangar-sized area, blindingly white with lights. He couldn't even guess how far below ground this massive room was, but he knew it must be deep inside the mountain. Electronic controls, computers, switches and testing equipment were banked along the white walls. He moved his gaze slowly until he had passed over the radiation-suited figures to the heart of the immense plant – the place where the separately gathered components had now been assembled into a small but obviously functional atomic device.

He stared at the assembled device, his eyes wide.

As he watched, an abrupt whistle blew through the huge arena scooped from the earth. The white-suited, helmeted engineers and scientists at work in the chamber where the atomic device had been assembled stopped working and lined up to exit the glass enclosed room within the larger plant.

Solo held his breath as the first man stepped through the double set of exit doors. Outside the chamber, they pulled off their helmets.

The impact was like a sharp karate blow in the face to Solo. One's mind could reel under the incredulous truth being revealed to him.

Abruptly, he remembered why the name of Broadmoor Rest had seemed so familiar to him from U.N.C.L.E. briefings. Again and again over the past two years, reports had come in from parts of the United States, Russia, France, Germany, records of scientists, engineers, physicists – all in sensitive missile work, each suffering mental breakdown, going to one sanitarium or another, but all, he now realized, eventually ending up here at Broadmoor Rest. Though the briefings had mentioned this place often enough to impress its title on his mind, there had been no concentrated reading of the names and professions of the men arriving here in an almost constant stream in the past twenty-four months.

He shook his head. Though often repeated, the idea of mentally ill men and their arrival at Broadmoor had not been noted in any context that would give it meaning – not until now. Those men had certainly been subjected to unnatural pressures, tensions and strains. Many of them crumpled under it, and it didn't add up to anything except the increased tempo of life in the atomic age. Men's minds and nerves snapped; they needed hospitalisation and treatment – Broadmoor Rest had been internationally respected as one of the best. These men had earned the best possible care; who would suspect they came here not because they were ill at all, but because they had sold out their governments, their families, their careers for the quick fortunes dangled before them by Thrush?

Because here they were.

Every face revealed to Solo by the removal of a helmet was familiar to him from the photos in the U.N.C.L.E. briefings. Every reputation was known to him, along with the facts of mental or nervous breakdown. Wolfang von Shisnagg, from the western zone of Germany, Kurt Helmeric, Pierre Curie de David – the whole long list of the brilliant engineers, scientists.

He slumped there for a long time, hidden in the

darkness of the abandoned incinerator shaft, watching the Who's Who of missile scientists pass by him. It took some moments for him to recover, he who had few illusions left concerning every man and his price.

VI

THE CHANGING of the shift continued. For a long time Solo remained where he was, watching the faces of those men who had sold out to Thrush.

The pattern was clear enough now – as well as the time. Early morning – doomsday!

He stirred, seeing how easily the mission would be accomplished. A plane would land on that strip out there, the bomb brought carefully up by lift – and flown to its target from well within the protective radar and early warning ring!

He slowly made his way back up the narrow shaft. Going up to the next level was a matter of muscle and patience: lift a foot, brace it and lift the other one without slipping or losing balance.

He stopped for a moment, exhausted, bracing himself as comfortably as he could in the dark chimney shaft. He placed the ear-plug against his ear, turning the barrel of the sound-detector upward in the passage, towards first one, then another branch of the chimney's interior complex.

He stayed some moments, listening. The aluminium cones picked up the sounds of persistent voices from above him, far to his left. The sounds were faint, but unlike any other throughout the entire complex at this early hour.

He inched towards that sound, using his elbows, his knees, his feet to worm himself forward. The sounds in the ear-plug increased until he was able to distinguish words and different male voices speaking.

He hesitated, thinking he could stay where he was in

safety and listen. But suddenly this was not good enough. He wanted to *see* those men engaged in an obviously high-level command meeting. Above him in the branch-passage he had followed was a patch of light – another unsealed fireplace.

He squirmed forward, his body aching with the pressures of the narrow confines, the inability to turn his head or tilt it more than a few inches.

The voices were loud now, and he removed the ear-plug, carefully placing the sound-detector behind him for fear the sound of metal against brick might betray his presence only feet away from these men in what must be, except for the chimney shaft, a soundproofed room.

When he had crawled to the grating, he saw that he was not going to be able to see the men in the room because a heavy mesh grating had been placed in front of the fireplace. He lay still, listening. He could hear what was going on in the room outside – the clash of voices, a glass set down on a tray, a fist slapping a palm – but he could see only dim shadows through the metallic grate.

One man was doing most of the talking.

Solo pressed forward, listening intently. It was a voice familiar to him. He wracked his brain trying to pin down that identity, but it eluded him.

Sam Su Yan's voice was easily identifiable: 'I don't agree that the plans to bomb Washington should be changed at this hour.'

'I'm sorry you don't agree, Sam. But you're going to have to do it my way. The decision is mine. I take every responsibility –'

'I am not interested in responsibility,' Su Yan said. 'All that interests me is success. I cannot conceive a greater success than dropping an atomic device on Washington, D.C. – and having the United States blame Russia for it. All diplomatic relations will be broken, and at least limited atomic war will break out, and both

Russia and the United States will be seriously weakened. Which will leave the balance of world power solely in the hands of Thrush. This was our plan from the first. We have built towards that moment, and you haven't yet given us a practical reason for altering our plans at this hour.'

'I've given you one unalterable reason. U.N.C.L.E. is not only suspicious: they have proof that a U.S. city is to be bombed so that the Russians will be blamed.'

'So, this agency is suspicious of this. What has this to do with our plans? You don't suggest delay – only a change of target.'

'Yes! I do! Waverly will alert Washington unless he hears from *both* the agents assigned to this matter. And you have already stated that you have those men detained – until after the delivery of our device –'

'That's right.'

'Then we cannot deliver it to Washington. The area is too sensitive, and as I say Waverly will alert the command there – he may already have done so.'

'Then what do you suggest?' Su Yan demanded, no suggestion of compromise hinted in his tone.

'The city that is struck is not important! Certainly Washington, D.C. would be a *coup* – nothing would please me better. But any important city will do – San Francisco, for instance; and think how easy this could be accomplished from here, and what perfect placement for settling the blame squarely upon the Russians. The U.S. government would see the strike as having somehow been accomplished over the Bering Strait, and no Russian denial would be tolerated!

'Besides, I have another objection to following through with the strike upon Washington. We have aimed towards that for two years – two years involving a great deal of planning, strategy, meetings, and all the work of collecting and smuggling in the components of our device. How many people have been entangled in all this? Whom can we trust? Am I to trust you though I've known you from childhood? Do you think I am deceived that you trust me – don't you know I'm aware that I am shadowed by operatives reporting to you, Su Yan?

'We have used the minds and skills of many engineers and scientists in assembling our device, preparing it for today's strike. All the more reason why we choose a different city – Chicago, New York, or why not Omaha itself, where the Strategic Air Command headquarters are?'

Su Yan's voice lowered. 'Agreed. I still believe that you're fretting yourself unnecessarily. You are forgetting our original premise. Civilian Defense warning systems have been blown in so many United States cities on the same day at the same hour for so many years that the people no longer react to them, or even consciously hear them any more. As long as our strike is made during the Civilian Defense warning time – in whatever city – it cannot fail.'

The other man – obviously San Yan's superior in this setup and more than faintly contemptuous of the Chinese-American – laughed. 'I know that. Even if those warning sirens were for real at that regular practise hour, no one would pay any attention until it was too late. The louder they wailed, the less heard by those sheep and goats. Those stupid creatures of habit would go about their normal lives – maybe complaining a little about the noise!'

'The city can be Washington!' Su Yan said, growing excited in contemplating the triumph, the same deceptive simplicity that had worked in the exploding lei used to kill one person. The same simplicity would be used to kill millions – on a gigantic scale, and using an atomic device.

Solo sweated, knowing that the scheme was so simple that it was foolproof. There was only one hope to counteract the awesome perfection of the simple scheme to use U.S. habit and its own defence warning system against itself. That hope was to alert the command in time.

He tilted his head, thinking he could follow the chimney shaft to a ground level opening somewhere, and somehow fight his way to freedom. It was all he could do, and there was no time to waste.

The voice of the leader in the room outside stopped him: 'I think you could ensure the success of his operation, Su Yan, simply by forcing the two agents to make calls to Waverly, assuring him there is no immediate danger and that they have joined forces and are working together.'

'Excellent,' Su Yan said. 'The one agent, Kuryakin, will require an injection to restore him to normality, but the other man can be handled easily – in fact, we are this moment working on him.'

Solo almost laughed, and then did not. There was a chill in Su Yan's tone, and he seemed to speak louder, as if he hoped to be overheard: 'It never occurred to Solo that we had his room and his suite on closed-circuit television. It seems to me he would have realized that in a place like this, all rooms are kept under surveillance.'

Solo began to inch away from the gate, stunned by the impact of Su Yan's boast. It had occurred to him that rooms of the inmates might be scanned through the big-brother device of closed-circuit television, but the very fact that the barred suite was far underground, and had apparently been used as a patient's room, had faked him off.

As he tried to move away, he remembered the almost incredibly easy way he had been permitted to escape to the field – like a mouse being tormented. What pleasure it must have given the watchers to see him build this sound-detector, to sort the parts dismantled by them.

They were laughing, but suddenly Solo was not. His arms refused to function; his legs no longer responded. He tried to move and he could not. He breathed deeply, conscious of the sweet scent of a gas, undoubtedly a nerve gas.

He lay there, conscious, but paralysed.

PART FOUR

INCIDENT THE MORNING
AFTER DOOMSDAY

I

IT WAS STILL early morning in the incredible ranges of the mountains where Broadmoor Rest crouched like an aerie of evil high upon its own promontory.

The hum of the fan-jet was picked up first. The battery of field lights flared to life, washing out the last grey wisps of night within the confines of the fieldstone walls.

The plane glided in with a grace and ease that communicated its perfection to the guards and the workers permitted in the area at this hour, and on this unusual day. A work of art always is a labour of love, and the most hardened armed man on the field could not deny the slight prickling of excitement he felt in seeing the way the plane touched down without a bump, jerk, or indecision.

The huge silver plane taxied up to the driveway nearest the main building of the sanitarium, was turned smoothly and headed into the wind. The engines died, the hatch was swung open, a ladder mechanically unfolded itself, and three men padded down the steps to the guards waiting to receive them on the runway.

The navigator was first, a slender man in his twenties,

an air-force navigation veteran. The co-pilot was French, a man who had more trouble with English syntax than with any plane that would lift its nose off the ground for him.

The pilot was the last man off the plane, and once he stepped out into the light, no one looked at anyone except him.

He paused on the top step a moment, glancing around, not as if he owned this plane – which he did not – or the sanitarium, but the world itself.

The man was well over six feet tall. He wore a flying jacket, freshly-pressed slacks and highly polished black shoes. His shirt was a blue-tinted imported linen. He was no longer young – he was somewhere in his forties, probably nine years older than he admitted even to himself. He had a record of flying on both sides in several wars on the African continent, of delivering arms to opposite camps on the same day, sometimes even the same flight. If one had money, one could buy him – until someone came along with more money.

'Let's get this show on the road,' he said to the head security officer. 'Where are the big wheels?' He grinned. 'The men with my orders – and my money.'

The security officer smiled with him because his smiling was infectious. It even made one overlook the padded bags under his dark, intense eyes, the only sign that he had been drinking heedlessly until an hour before flight time this morning. His breath was still liquor-tart, but he was completely cold and in command of himself.

'I was told to inform you, Mr. Baker,' the security officer said. 'There may be a slight delay.'

Baker stopped smiling. 'The hell with that, Charley. Take me to your leader. There's no delay on this boat. We get off on the minute or we don't go.'

'I'm just telling what I was ordered to tell you–'

'And I'm just countermanding your orders, Ace,' Baker said. 'Let's go give the words to the wheels.'

'They may not like being interrupted—'

Baker lost his temper instantly. His voice rasped, and the security guard, larger and heavier, paled slightly and retreated. He didn't like looking at what he saw in those dark eyes, so full of laughter an instant before.

'To hell with what they like, Ace,' Baker said. 'They can't delay this. It's on, it's on schedule. Or it's off. It takes a fan-jet a certain number of hours to go X number of miles. They know as well as I do, the timing has to be perfect. Come on. Take me to them, and I'll lay the word on them.'

II

SOLO'S MIND remained entirely clear, but his body was numbed, incapable of movement.

He lay there exploring the simplicity of this plan: death from the most unexpected source. From lovely ginger flowers formed into a brilliant, scented lei. And from the clear noon sky during a civilian defence test alert. The more one heard the scream of those accustomed sirens, the less one was impressed – hadn't they wailed last night at the same hour, and every week for the past ten years?

In his fevered mind, Solo saw that atomic device, painstakingly assembled by the finest minds Thrush's money and threats and blackmail could buy, waiting down there to be hoisted on that open lift to the plane at ground-level.

He twisted frantically, but all the writhing was inside his skin, in his mind.

All this whirled through Solo's thoughts as he heard Su Yan order the grating removed from the fireplace of the command room.

When the grate was removed, Solo stared for a moment at the faces of the guards bending down to drag him out. Then, beyond them, he saw the cabinets along the walls, the filing cases, realising that this room was the heart of the Thrush operations at this base.

'One never knows what sort of animal one will find in one's walls, eh?' Su Yan said. His voice mocked at Solo. 'Pull it out, and we'll exterminate it.'

The guards caught Solo by the shirt collar and by the hair, pulling him into the room.

They dropped him less than carefully upon the tiled flooring. Solo lay sprawled where he struck, helpless even to straighten his twisted arm. For all intents and purposes, his body was dead; only his mind persisted alive.

He heard Su Yan chuckle. 'Dirty beast, isn't he? Covered with soot and grime. I'm afraid he's not exactly the sort of Santa Claus from a chimney I've always imagined.'

From where he had been dropped Solo could see only a small portion of the room. His mind was tormented with the seeds of madness: he knew of the awesome plan to destroy civilization, and he could not even move a muscle of his hands or feet. And time ticked away.

Time stood still then for a moment when there was a sharp rapping on the door.

Su Yan strode across the room and opened it. Solo heard anger and outrage in his voice as he demanded, 'What are you doing in here?'

A hesitant voice said, 'It's Colonel Baker, sir. He says he either talks to you people, or he flies out – I thought you'd want to know.'

'What's the hush-hush?' Baker strode into the room, pushing the door out of Su Yan's grasp. 'You people don't intimidate me. Put a bullet in me, pay me off, or keep the schedule. It's all the same to me.'

'What's eating you, Baker?' The head of the operations spoke now, and Solo fought to lift his head enough to see him.

Baker laughed. 'I'll tell you what's eating me, Wheel. You people hired me on a trick that sounded good because it offered a challenge to me. You know? Pin-pointed. Precisely timed. Well, I'm here and there's talk of delay. My plane can travel only so fast – there's so much distance to cover, and precise timing won't wait. Either follow through with the plans – and that means keeping to an exact schedule – or pay me off. Real simple. No sweat. Nothing to get excited about.'

III

THE EXCITEMENT WAS quickly quelled, the room cleared for the moment except for Su Yan and the man U.N.C.L.E. had known for so long only as Tixe Ylno. There was no doubt now. This was the biggest wheel of all in Operation Doomsday.

'The pilot was absolutely right, Su Yan,' Tixe Ylno was saying. 'The difference of a few minutes would spoil the arrival of the device as the test sirens started in our target area. One cannot help admiring Colonel Baker. He has stayed alive to this moment by being sure of everything he does connected with flying.'

Su Yan was not impressed. 'He's not the kind of man I'd care to have in the sort of world I envision after today.'

Tixe Ylno laughed. 'It's highly unlikely that Colonel Baker will survive the holocaust, old friend. Those of us here underground may be the only ones to see the end of this conflict.'

Tixe Ylno paced across the room, stood staring down at Solo sprawled like a rag doll on the chilled flooring.

Solo's eyes widened. He felt the nausea and sickness spread inside his numbed body. He no longer needed the code name for Tixe Ylno.

The man standing over him was Osgood DeVry, the president's adviser and confidante.

DeVry stared down at him a moment, his face without any expression. Then he spoke across his shoulder. 'Get

133

Kuryakin and the girl in here. There's no more time for delay.'

'I'll bring them myself,' Sam Su Yan said from across the room. 'We'll want Dr. Calyort to give him an injection before we get him in here.'

DeVry waved his hand impatiently.

The corridor door whispered open, sighed closed, and Solo was alone with DeVry.

DeVry's face twisted into a contemptuous smile, staring down at Solo. 'You can stop looking at me with such astonishment and revulsion, Solo. It won't help you to know my true identity. Believe me, you'd never have been permitted to see me, or even hear my voice, except that you're slated for immediate oblivion.'

He prowled away, then returned. He said, 'I cannot tell you how much I've enjoyed all these months reading the classified and confidential reports your agency has been making on me under my code name of Tixe Ylno. The very name itself amused every time I saw it – because I do plan exit only for the two great powers of this earth.'

DeVry glanced at his watch, shooting his cuff, and then shaking it down over his wrist.

'The president trusted you – almost more than any other man on earth,' Solo said, somewhat astonished that he could speak coherently, though his body remained in a state of paralysis.

'I'm not interested in sentimentality, or the mistakes other men make simply because they see in you some quality they possess in themselves.'

'You're one of the most influential men in this country. What is it going to buy you to destroy it?'

DeVry smiled at him coldly. 'It's going to buy me what I need.'

'Do you need a world destroyed by an atomic war?'

'At the moment, I do. For many reasons. Most of them you wouldn't even understand. You say I'm influential as a presidential flunkey? I shall be a great deal more influential in the world that remains – I shall dictate all its terms.'

'You may be talking to yourself.'

DeVry appeared unmoved by this possibility.

'If I am,' he replied, 'I shall tell myself that I have what a man of pride must have. Vindication. Revenge for the wrongs compounded upon me, and which I've had to take until I simply cannot take them any more.'

Solo stared at the man, wondering what had happened to him to cause his mind to break like this – because he saw that DeVry was insane, no longer able to conceive the horror of a world blasted by atomic radiation. What had happened to this man so long trusted and respected by his close friend, the president?

DeVry answered this for him, too. 'I tried to warn him. The president – I tried to warn him. He just laughed, and slapped me on the back and wouldn't listen. Well, he'll listen now. I told them I wanted a position worthy of my talents, the sort of post I had earned all these years in military and political life. They pick my brains. Then let them put me in a position where I'd be respected for the decisions I either make or influence. Years ago, I was promised the job that I would have taken, would have executed better than it has ever been handled, and would have been contented with. They promised me that I would head Central Intelligence. I even spoke about it to my close friends, relatives. I was filled with pride and satisfaction. It was what I wanted.'

DeVry strode out of the perimeter of Solo's vision, and then after a moment walked restlessly back.

'I was rated a security risk! Do you hear that? I was rated a security risk. The very fact that I was a security risk triggered a witch-hunt in Washington that dug down to the levels of generals, colonels, and majors in all the branches of the military! Me. Every day, half my life devoted, sacrificed, spent on behalf of the president, and through him this stupid, senseless, ungrateful country.

135

Make a profit. Make a profit. Use all influential power –
and discard those who don't have it.

'Sure, the president kept me on. Politics demanded it.
Security demanded it. And I was his friend. But I was
now classified as a security risk, and doors that had
always been open to me were suddenly closed. Now,
after twenty-five years of sacrifice, I was nothing more
than a flunkey fetching coffee and bringing in non-
classified notes.

'I was a risk – and I could not have the job I wanted
more than anything on earth, the job that the president
himself had promised me. I had made one mistake – one
bad judgment, years before – and it doomed me, no
matter how loyal I'd been in all the years since then, no
matter how hard I had worked!

'Well, I am a man of pride, and I cannot live with that
wrong. It will be avenged!'

'Thank God you didn't get the post as head of the
C.I.A.' Solo said fervently.

DeVry strode towards him. Solo saw the rage swirl in
his eyes, saw the terrible self-control the man exercised
to keep from kicking him in the face. His foot lifted,
trembled, and his mouth worked.

After a moment DeVry spoke calmly. 'Well, it doesn't
matter. The C.I.A. won't mean much after today, Mr.
Solo.'

IV

SOLO WATCHED DeVry turn as a door whispered open
across the room.

Barbry entered first. Solo could see her face. She
looked ill with fright. Her cheeks were pallid, and her
eyes were wild, like some frantic animal's.

Illya stepped in next. His gaze flew about the room,
sizing it up, and then he saw Solo. He forgot Su Yan,
DeVry, the guards. He crossed the room swiftly,

kneeling beside Solo.

'You're alive,' Illya's voice conveyed his relief.

'Just about,' Solo said.

'A temporary condition for the three of you,' Su Yan said.

A guard caught Illya by the collar and jerked him around.

Illya came upward on his toes, and kept turning, bringing his extended hand upwards into the guard's stomach. The man gave a little sob of agony and bent double, dropping his gun.

Illya lunged for it, and Su Yan permitted him to get his hands on it before he karate-chopped him across the neck. Illya plunged straight down, landing hard on his face, his arms thrust out before him.

'Heroics,' Su Yan said in contempt. 'A kind of illness with these people.'

'If you've killed him before he makes that call to his superior,' Osgood DeVry said, 'you may live to regret your own heroics.'

Su Yan frowned slightly, then shook his head. 'No. I'll call Dr. Calyort in and have him happy to talk in minutes.'

But as Su Yan turned towards the telephone on the conference table, lights flashed and then dimmed. Su Yan and DeVry straightened, glancing at each other.

'The device is being removed to the lift,' Su Yan said. 'We have flight time to make the call.'

The two guards left the room ahead of DeVry. The man whom Illya had attacked still walked slightly doubled over, but carried his weapon again.

Su Yan lifted Illya, placed him in a chair, secured his hands behind him and left him there, unconscious.

'I'm afraid we have bad news for you, Solo,' Su Yan said. 'We have reached the decision that you are expendable – ahead of the operation. We need only the voice of one of you, and we have determined that Kuryakin, despite his tendency to reckless acts, will be

137

the easiest to control. I hope you will believe me when I tell you how sorry I am that I won't be seeing you again.'

Solo did not speak, watching him.

Su Yan caught Barbry by the arm, leading her towards one of the cylinders lined on the far wall. Watching them, Solo saw how the nerve gas had been pumped to him through a small rubber tubing that ran along the baseboard to the fireplace.

'A nerve gas here that should interest you, Solo,' Su Yan said. He paused when the lights dimmed again. 'Developed by our own scientists and chemists. The effect is much like that of hypnosis. The subject remains in a waking-sleep state, as in hypnosis. As in hypnosis she is not aware of what she is doing while she is under its effects. And unlike hypnosis, the so-called moral-censor is not at work. The subject follows only those orders given her while she is going under – and there is not the danger of morals or conscience as a deterrent. She is literally unable to do anything except follow those orders. I'm sure this is going to prove most interesting to you.

The lights dimmed again and Su Yan hurried himself slightly. When Barbry opposed him, trying to break free, he drew his arm back and almost struck her. At the last moment he controlled his rage. Instead of hitting her, he simply stared down at her and spoke no more than three or four whispered words. Barbry no longer offered any resistance.

He sat her down in a chair beside one of the cylinders. He placed a rubber cap firmly over her mouth and nose, holding it in place. He turned the valve on the cylinder. There was a whisper of sound, the sibilant hiss of gas.

Solo strained to move his body, but found himself still in that state of physical paralysis. He saw that Su Yan was not using this same gas on Barbry.

His low voice struck at Barbry. 'I am going to leave a knife with you, Barbry. Do you understand?'

138

Solo saw that the girl's eyes were open. There was no longer any terror in them. Her blinking seemed to indicate to Su Yan that she still heard him, still understood him. He glanced at the needle on the cylinder gauge.

Satisfied that the flow of gas was slow, steady, adequate, Su Yan spoke again. 'When I am out of the room, Barbry, you will kill Napoleon Solo there on the floor. You will strike between the shoulder blades. Once. Twice. Three times. You will make certain he is dead before you use the knife on yourself. You will drive the knife upwards through your solar plexus into your heart.'

Solo, in horror, heard Su Yan calmly repeat these instructions in the same unemotional tone. He could see Barbry's face, and he saw there was no recoiling, no revulsion in her eyes. He could not tell if she understood Su Yan, but the thin, tall man appeared satisfied. He reached over and turned off the valve; the whispering hiss of gas ceased.

He stood another moment with the rubber cap in place over Barbry's nose and mouth. Then he set the cup in its holder. He drew a glitteringly sharp knife from his inner jacket pocket. He placed it firmly in Barbary's grasp, folding her fingers over the handle, pressing them closed, watching her narrowly as he worked.

Su Yan stepped back and Barbry sat there, staring straight ahead, the knife clasped firmly in her fist.

Su Yan watched her a moment and then nodded, apparently satisfied. The building lights dimmed again. He turned, moving towards the door, paused, glancing at Solo on the floor.

'Goodbye, Mr. Solo,' Su Yan stared at him. 'If it will comfort you, I can assure you that you and Esther Kappmyer will be found dead in your room at the St. Francis Hotel.'

'Somehow there's no comforting thought there,' Solo said.

'When it happens,' Su Yan said, 'Washington, D.C. will be only atomic rubble, and World War III will be under way.'

'Too bad you haven't reason enough left to see what will happen when hydrogen bombs are used.'

Su Yan had turned towards the door; now he heeled around angrily.

'We can build well on the ruin of this world – and small loss. Other civilizations have grown out of the rubble of those before them.'

'If you say so.'

'Don't fight it so,' Su Yan said with a chilled smile. 'You have the comforting thought that you gave your life in an heroic effort to avert what you see as a catastrophe.'

Now Solo laughed. 'I wonder what comforting thought you will find, Su Yan, when you finally realise that the catastrophe is more immense than your imagination can contain – when there is nothing left for you to rule? I've always wondered what thoughts are comforting to an international fink.'

Su Yan gripped the door until his knuckles whitened. Obviously he fought a battle against his fiery desire to stride back across the room and finish off Solo.

Whatever he might have done, the thought was wiped away as the lights dimmed one more time. He glanced, as if for the final check, at Solo helpless on the floor, at Illya bound and unconscious in a straight chair, and Barbry seated with that gleaming six-inch knife gripped tightly in her fist.

This still-life pleased him entirely, and he gave a small nod of satisfaction before he stepped through the door and closed it behind him.

The thundering of noises rumbled through the air ducts under the ceiling of the room. Forcing himself to keep his gaze away from Barbry and the knife in her hand, Solo concentrated on the cabinets along the far walls, seeing weaponry, masks and ammunition as well

140

as cylinders of several types of gases. Every attack weapon he would need to stop DeVry and Su Yan – only feet away from him, and yet they might as well have been on the dark side of the moon.

Barbry stirred, and Solo jerked his eyes back to her. The chair scraped as she stood up.

He said, keeping his voice level, unemotional. 'Don't move, Barbry. Stay where you are.'

She stood up slowly, her gaze fixed on his vulnerable back. She stared at him, but he knew that she had not heard a word he had said. She was conditioned against any thought except that of murder and suicide implanted in her mind by Samuel Su Yan.

V

FOLLOWED BY two guards, Su Yan strode along the corridor to the elevator marked *Private*. He stepped into it and, with his guards, slipped quickly down into the white-walled laboratory where the atomic device had been assembled and was now being loaded for the upward ride to the field where it would be placed in the bomb-bay of the sleek silver fan-jet.

As Su Yan left the elevator, he saw only one man in the metallically lighted area who seemed relaxed. This was Colonel Baker, the renegade pilot who had hired-out to make delivery, as specified, of one atomic device.

Su Yan stared at the man; he lounged, drinking a beer, while his payload was being painstakingly carted via narrow rail over the seventy or eighty feet of floor-space to the specially rigged open elevator.

Su Yan wondered if the arrogant adventurer had looked beyond that moment when he would dump his atomic payload as contracted.

Su Yan's mouth twisted. There was not the least doubt in his mind that Colonel Baker would make the delivery. It was more than the flat fee of one million dollars that was to be paid before the plane took off this morning. It was the challenge that would carry Baker through that strike. The tougher the going got for him at the zero-hour, the greater would be the flier's determination and pleasure in making the strike.

Still, Su Yan wondered what sort of irresponsible man the colonel had to be to miss the most important aspect of the whole matter. He was going to have a million dollars – but where was he going to spend it? Perhaps he had thought of that, and maybe the promise of one more war fought in the air had outweighed all other considerations for him. No one would ever know what he was thinking as he stood, richly tailored, immaculate, and still slightly hung over, awaiting the fateful loading of his biggest payload.

Su Yan walked to the place where Osgood DeVry stood with several other men – scientists, engineers, technicians, guards, all inspecting the manually-operated series of winches, cables and chains that would operate the open lift.

Su Yan told himself that DeVry was going to find fault, and he was not disappointed.

'What's wrong with electric power to operate the lift?' he asked. 'They run all the other elevators.'

Su Yan pointed, with infinite Oriental patience, at the small ratchet turning with each click of the smallest wheel in the series. 'The lift can be operated from here with the touch of a finger. Another flick of the smallest finger drops this ratchet into the cog wheels, instantly stopping the lift. We can know what's happening down here, but not above. We had to prepare for every contingency – including attack, power-failure, accident. The engineers must have warned you that this atomic device is jerry-built to say the least. We have tried to measure to the least decibel the amount of sound or movement that might activate it, but it is only an educated guess. We are handling it with every care until we get it loaded on your pilot's plane. After that,' Su

Yan shrugged. 'Delivery is his problem.'

Colonel Baker laughed. 'Load it up, Ace. I've delivered eggs through hurricanes without breaking one of them.'

VI

SOLO'S FRANTIC mind ordered every muscle in his body to move – any movement at all. Watching Barbry rise from her chair with the knife gleaming in her taut fist, he felt his senses boil as adrenalin coursed into his bloodstream.

His order was not a complete failure. But the response he did elicit was worse than failing, more demoralizing.

Wasn't there faint movement, return of life to his toes? He stared at his fingers, seeing them flex, but nothing more than a tremor. It was slow, too slow, like the movement of that part of an iceberg below the surface of some frozen sea.

Operation Doomsday continued unchecked. The noises from below came like taunting sounds from the channels of the air ducts: the pulse of engines, the distant turn of metal wheels on iron tracks, the whirring rasps of winches and cables.

Across the room, Illya stirred, straightening his head from his shoulder. He came awake painfully slowly. At first when Solo cried out his name, Illya didn't respond, still too drugged with pain and dulled with his forced sleep.

'Illya! Listen to me!'

Across the room, Illya sat straighter, a flicker of light showing in his eyes. Solo called out again, urgently.

'Illya. Wake up, Illya!'

Illya stirred, his head came up and his eyes focused. He saw Barbry, the gleaming knife, the direction of her intent gaze, and read in that instant the grave danger to Solo.

143

He tried to come up off the chair, but the bonds stopped him, yanking him back down. The chair scraped on the tile flooring, but not even this sudden sound penetrated Barby's consciousness.

She did not even hear it.

'Barbry!' Illya called. 'Barbry. Over here!'

It was no good. She did not hear his voice any more than she had heard the abrupt scraping of his chair. As far as Barbry knew in that moment, only she, Solo, the knife and her orders to kill existed.

Barbry walked towards Solo slowly, with the careful, wooden manner of a sleepwalker.

She raised the knife to shoulder-level and she kept it there as she walked.

She was looking fixedly at Solo. Solo told himself there was infinite sadness in those deep violet eyes. But common sense warned him this was illusion. Her gaze was intent upon him, but there was no emotion in it – the intense concentration was upon that vulnerable place where she'd strike with that knife between his shoulder blades.

'She can't kill like this – even in hypnosis!' Illya said, working with the bonds securing his wrists.

'She's not in hypnosis,' Solo said, wriggling his fingers, squirming his toes within his shoes, sweating because the return of his senses was slow, too slow. 'It's a nerve gas. She's like a robot, programmed to kill, and that's all she knows.'

'They haven't missed a trick,' Illya said, struggling.

Solo stared at Illya on that chair. Like the weaponry in the cabinets, Illya was so near, yet impossibly far away.

He saw Illya interpret the question in his eyes. Could he break out of those fetters in time?

Illya made no effort to deceive him. He shook his head. Though his wrists bled, he could not work his hands free, not in time.

Time. Solo saw the next fateful step made by the feet

144

shod in patent-leather pumps, high heels, the trim ankles. He did not look higher; he was staring at Illya, at the cabinets of weaponry. Illya was not going to work free in time to stop Barbry. But perhaps this wasn't as important as what he might accomplish when he was free.

Illya at least had a chance to alert U.N.C.L.E in time to avert an international catastrophe. Even if he, Solo, died here, Illya still could make it.

Solo pitched his voice at an unemotional level, staring at Illya. 'No matter what happens, to me and to Barbry, don't let it slow you down. Right now, below us, they're loading an atomic device that will be dropped on Washington, D.C. The destruction there will be tremendous – but it will only be the beginning, if it starts an atomic war.

'There are some things you must do, Illya. In order to accomplish them, find the camera eye of the closed-circuit television in this room. Smash it. Then arm yourself from that row of cabinets. Somehow you've got to get out of here, and somehow you've got to get word to Waverly. Time has run out, Illya. They're loading the device right now.'

'I'll do it,' Illya said. His voice shook with the savagery of his working to free himself.

Solo felt the toe of a sleek slipper strike his face. He stared at the shoe, and with the inconsistency that occurs in moments of extreme danger, he realised that he could see his reflection in the slick surface of those slippers – his helpless body mirrored there.

It occurred to him that he could watch himself being killed.

He felt his pulses quicken, the increased beat of his heart, the adrenalin fed uselessly into his system. All his senses were keenly alert to this final danger. But he was unable to move.

She stood above him a moment, not moving because she had walked as far as she could.

The lights in the room dimmed, flickered. A new sound raged up through the air ducts. Solo recognized it because he had been listening for it. The large elevator, especially constructed for this one mission, was slowly grinding into motion, lifting the atomic device to ground level.

Solo shivered – not with fear, but rage at his helplessness.

That plane would soon be airborne, loaded with its deadly cargo. It didn't seem to matter much now that a girl named Barbry Coast was bending over him, ready to drive a knife into his back. What mattered was that the entire world was in danger, and he could do nothing to stop it.

There was a new and terrible irony in it, too. Life now quivered tentatively more than halfway down his fingers. He could wriggle his feet, but he could not lift them. He could flex his fingers, but he could not move his hands.

Using all his will power, he managed to turn his neck, his head twisting so that he faced Barbry. There was nothing to see in her face except the pallid emptiness.

'Barbry!'

She did not respond. He saw that her eyes did not even blink. Nothing would reach her.

He sweated, seeing the knife lifting above her shoulder, her gaze fixed on his back, between his shoulder blades, precisely as Su Yan had commanded her.

Below them, the rumble of the slowly rising lift.

Nearer, the easy breathing as Barbry lifted the knife to plunge it – three times, Su Yan had told her. She was totally relaxed, dispassionate, her subconscious entirely divorced from this robot-action of her body.

The lifting elevator grumbled, the building quivering.

The knife glittered, stopping at the crest of the arc. The blade, zeroing on Solo's heart, quivered in her hand, ready to flash downwards.

Solo tensed, desperately ordering his arm to fling upwards – but knowing in advance that it wasn't going to do it.

VII

SOLO HEARD the rustle of movement, the sudden shout of warning. For a split second he lay still, then his legs moved, and he twisted to one side. He swung his arm upwards, and the tingling sensation of returning life flushed through him.

He saw the knife striking downward. But contact was never made. Illya lunged through the air in an impossibly long tackle. He did it expertly, too, Solo saw, because to hit Barbry and drive her down upon him would sent that knife into him with an impact Barbry could never manage alone.

But Illya struck low, driving upwards from the balls of his feet. His driving tackle carried Barbry forward and up, sending her sailing across Solo's body to the tiled flooring beyond him.

It was a near thing, but it was a complete miss. She struck face down, sliding some feet, losing the knife so that it clattered away almost to the wall.

Illya landed on top of Solo, rolling across him. Solo saw that his wrists and his shirt were streaked with his blood, but his hands and arms were free.

Solo spoke at once, putting the danger from Barbry and her knife from his mind, computing ahead, forcing himself to remain cool. He could move his head now, and his gaze located the lens of the closed-circuit camera in the far wall.

Before Illya could pull himself around, Solo was speaking to him in a low tone: 'The camera eye is directly across there, high in the wall. If you smash it, the control room will know it instantly.'

Illya was on his feet. His gaze found the camera eye.

He crossed the room, shoving a chair to the wall. Standing on the chair, he placed his hand over the lens and then calmly unscrewed it from the camera. Turning it around, he jammed it hard back into the aperture.

He leaped off the chair.

Solo said, 'Illya. Stop her.'

Barbry had pulled herself to her feet. Still moving in that halting robot's motion, she crossed to the wall and retrieved the knife.

'A lady with a one-way mind,' Illya said.

He strode across the room. She stared vacantly at him. He tried to take the knife, but she resisted. He caught her wrist and twisted it, removing the knife from her grasp. Her faced showed no pain.

'She's disarmed,' Illya said across his shoulder. 'But I'm afraid she still has murder on her mind.'

Solo was sitting up now. He was not sure that he could stand, or that his legs would support him if he made it, but tension and rage had sent blood pulsing through his body, nullifying the effects of the paralysing gas.

He pulled himself up by clinging to a table, exploring the slow, confused return of his sensations. His skin tingled as a hand or fingers might, held too long in one position, or if the circulation were cut off.

He stood shakily, like a new-born colt, clinging to the highly polished blond table.

He heard the continued whine of the elevator, the rumbling through the earth and the foundations of the building.

He straightened as a *woup-woup* whistling of the warning sirens flared, and then continued through the building. He knew the wrecked closed-circuit TV camera had created this warning. Undoubtedly word was already being called to DeVry and Su Yan below them.

'Illya,' Solo said, keeping the warning sounds out of his thought processes. 'Help me.'

Illya ran to him. Solo jerked his head towards the gas

cylinders.

Solo was able to move only with a slow, shuffling walk that enraged him.

He forced himself to speak calmly, but inside he was shaking desperately with the fear of failure even when he'd been given this last chance.

'Three gas masks from that cabinet, Illya. A machine pistol from there. Watch that door. If it opens, start firing, and keep firing until it closes – no matter who it is.'

Illya nodded.

Solo pulled free and half-fell against the wall where the rubber tubing which had carried the nerve gas to him still lay. He picked up the tubing, disconnected it from the cylinder of nerve gas, and reconnected it to one of a simple anaesthetic gas. Then he ran the rubber tubing up the wall to the air conditioning duct.

Illya broke open the cabinets. He tossed a gas mask to Solo, pulled one over his own head. With a machine pistol under his arm, he crossed the room to where Barbry stood as though dazed, or walking in her sleep.

Solo waited only until the mask was being pulled down over Barbry's head. He turned the cut-on valve of the anaesthetic cylinder to full.

He stared at the gauge, seeing the needle flash across it, and danger lights flare red. The lights he ignored, just as he ignored the increased *woup-woup* of the warning whistle.

The faint whispering of an opening door struck him and he turned at the moment Illya, on his knees, pressed the trigger of the machine pistol.

Two guards were already running into the room. The machine-pistol bucked, and they crumpled forwards, still running after they were already dead.

Shuffling, pulling himself along the cabinets, Solo armed himself. The door was pulled closed.

'Don't try to wait for me,' Solo told Illya. 'Try to stop that elevator – even if you have to detonate their bomb.'

He saw Illya nod inside his gas mask.

Illya gave Barbry a shove. She stumbled, moving towards Solo. He caught her, gripping her arm with his left hand.

Illya stepped over the bodies of the dead guards. He emptied the machine pistol into the electrically-controlled lock mechanism of the door. It swung open like the broken wing of a bird.

Illya tossed the emptied machine pistol behind him. Solo tossed him two new guns, and Illya went through the door into the corridor. The *woup-wouping* whistle was increased ten times with the thick door hanging open.

Through the din, Solo heard the rasping fire of the machine pistol outside the door.

He heard DeVry's voice blaring on the suddenly activated building intercom. 'Proceed! Proceed! Proceed! Do not stop for anything! Proceed with the plan as scheduled! Do not stop! Proceed! Proceed!'

There was wildness in his voice, and frustration, and the brittle wail of insanity as the anaesthetic gas spread through the air-conditioning and men hesitated in what they were doing, paused, stopped, and sank to the floor unconscious.

DeVry's voice persisted.

The intercom crackled with his commands, with his shouting, his cursing, his sobbing.

Solo grabbed Barbry's arm, dragging her after him.

He stared at her face through the plastic face-shield of her mask. Her violet eyes remained staring, drugged. He talked to her savagely, knowing she was not hearing him, but himself gathering some strength from bullying her into following him from the room.

In the corridor outside, Illya was the first person he saw. The young agent held his machine pistol at the ready, but Solo saw in his face through the mask that Illya was lost.

'The elevators,' Solo said. 'The one marked private

must go down to the underground lab.'

'Come on,' Illya said. 'We'll go together. There's time now. The gas has hit this place hard.'

Solo moved with him, still shuffling, still dragging Barbry after him. He saw men slumped against the walls, lying on the flooring, some of them with guns fallen from their limp hands.

He saw something else. This was Illya's show from this moment. He could shuffle along in his wake, he could fire his machine pistol, he could find their way through the maze of floors and corridors – but only Illya could move with any speed.

They reached the elevators. DeVry's voice was weaker, but his wails were higher-pitched. Illya pressed the button on the elevator marked *Private*. When it whirred to a stop, its doors parting, they saw two guards slumped on the cage flooring, guns beside them.

Illya pressed the last button on the panel. The elevator started a swift descent. DeVry's voice rose, faded on the intercom, sank to a whisper, ceased. . . .

The elevator doors parted on the huge white-lighted lab. The manually operated elevator was high above their level. The man operating it had donned one of the masks the scientists used inside the atomic cages. He had oxygen and protection from the anaesthetic.

Otherwise the huge room was like a place of human statues. Men in almost every position, caught there in that final moment when the gas had felled them. Men with guns in their arms, men fallen to their knees or braced against walls. Colonel Baker, the renegade pilot, still clung to his can of beer, even in unconsciousness. Sam Su Yan had been struck to his knees. Across the room at the intercom microphone, DeVry still clutched the instrument on his knees before its lighted panel.

The lift operator jerked his head up, and saw Illya run out of the elevator ahead of Solo and Barbry.

The operator instinctively slapped at the braking-ratchet on the smallest series of wheels. As his fingers struck the small metal piece, Illya shot him. He toppled away from the controls.

The tiny ratchet fell downwards, slipping between the cogs of the oiled wheels. But total contact had not been made. The small wheel slipped past the ratchet. It struck the next cog, slowing it. But the second larger wheel then slipped backwards, not braked, and so on in a series until the cables lifting the hoist slipped and the elevator shuddered, slipping downwards each time the ratchet missed its cog.

Illya stared at the small wheels a moment, then at the trembling cables under the flooring of the lift.

'Let's get out of here! That hoist will fall faster and faster – by the time it strikes this sump–'

He did not even bother to finish the thought, herding Solo and Barbry ahead of him into the elevator. He stopped at the doors, holding them open. He lifted his machine pistol, aiming it at Sam Yu San, meaning to kill him and DeVry before he cleared out.

'Forget it!' Solo said behind him. 'When that lift falls out of control, their bomb is going to go. Let them go with it.'

The breath sighed out of him and Illya nodded. he stared one final time at Su Yan, at DeVry across the room, at that little ratchet slipping as it tried to brake that tiny wheel.

He let the gun sink to his side.

The elevator doors whispered shut. The warning whistle continued to wail in the eerie world of immobility. The elevator screamed upwards, stopping at ground level.

'Nobody outside this building is going to be affected by that gas,' Solo warned. 'Be ready to fight your way out.'

Illya nodded. 'I need no coaxing. The way that ratchet is slipping is all the impetus I need for clearing out of here, fast, no matter who's in my way.'

Solo led them along the corridor to the maintenance

exit, out of which he had been permitted to run in his earlier escape attempt. Su Yan had enjoyed that cat-and-mouse game, letting him get almost within reach of escape, but that dry run had shown him where the institute cars were parked.

He shoved open the door, hearing the savage yelping of the dogs from the kennel. He and Barbry stepped out into the bright morning sunlight, followed by Illya with his gun held at the ready.

The first car Solo saw on the ramp was a Rolls-Royce, black, gleaming, headed out on the drive. It was undoubtedly Osgood DeVry's car, waiting for an instant getaway in case of any disruption in the plans of the doomsday bomb.

Beyond the garage and the cars on the ramp, the silver fan-jet rested in the sun, surrounded by armed men and technicians. The *woup-wouping* whistle shattered the morning silence.

'The Rolls.' Solo said. 'If any car has a chance to clear this place, it would be DeVry's.'

They ran for it. Inside the garage, men shouted. Illya grabbed the door of the Rolls, threw it open. In the same motion, he knelt, the machine pistol bucking and rattling as he spray-fired into the garage.

Men turned, running from the plane. Illya sprang into the Rolls under the wheel, turning the key as he moved. Solo thrust Barbry in between them, and Illya had the car rolling as he struck the seat and slammed the door.

The men on the grass sank to their knees, firing at the racing car. Illya braced the machine pistol on the window, firing only for effect. His entire attention was on the drive and the iron gate in the fieldstone walls.

The gate attendant ran out as the car approached. Behind him, Solo saw the other cars being started, racing forwards in pursuit.

Illya held the machine pistol out in plain sight, fixed on the guard. He shouted at him. The man nodded quickly pressing a button. The huge gates swung open.

Illya stepped hard on the gas. 'I've always loved the way these things look,' he said. 'But they handle awkwardly.'

Solo was watching the road behind them. 'Do you suppose you could move it faster?'

'I don't know,' Illya replied. 'I've never actually driven one before.'

He held the car close to the inside of the winding mountain road, slowing as he went into the curves, but speeding as he navigated them.

They were some miles down the mountain when the explosion came. It shook the earth, battering it. From above them, earth crumpled and boulders larger than houses fell free. Other small explosions followed. Behind them there was silence as the pursuing cars stopped up above.

'That chalet up there,' Illya said, shivering slightly. 'It must have crumbled into itself.'

'An underground atomic explosion that they'll pick up all over the world,' Solo said. He drew the mask off his face. 'Maybe they'll write it off as an earthquake.'

The battered mountain continued to quiver and shake as if torn loose from its foundations. The violence of that atomic underground blast loosened the earth from its shackles. Huge boulders, torn loose, hurtled downwards like pebbles in a land-pounding avalanche. Brittle-rooted trees broke out of the rocky soil, sending up more thunder, more dust.

The big car rattled to its underpinnings. It lunged out of control and, with the convulsions torturing the earth, danced in jerky pirouettes from one side of the narrow road to the other. Shatterproof glass splintered, webbed and crumpled.

Illya fought the wheel, pulling his foot off the accelerator.

His hands gripped the wheel even harder when there was an electronically triggered click, and Su Yan's voice rose eerily from a concealed recorder.

'Memo,' the voice droned. 'From Samuel Su Yan to Osgood DeVry.' The car slowed. 'Well, old friend of childhood days – whom I trusted no more then than now – you will be hearing this memo for one reason only. Something will have fouled our plan, and you will be running for safety, leaving me to face the debacle. This time you won't make it'–'

As if sharing the same thought, Solo and Illya simultaneously thrust open doors on both sides of the Rolls.

The voice continued, 'Race down the mountain. The heat bomb will be triggered by your speed. You can't win. I always have the last word. It's too late for you now – and my last word, my friend, is goodbye.'

The recording was speaking to an empty car.

Solo grabbed Barbry's head against his chest and hurtled them outwards. When Illya leaped free the car went finally out of control. As it struck a mountain wall and rebounded, the heat bomb exploded, turning the mountain white. The fragmented car still moved, rolling, brightly orange with flames, to the brink of the cliff, and over it.

The Man From U.N.C.L.E.

by

Michael Avallone

In Utangaville, Africa, it took two days. In Spayerwood, Scotland, it happened overnight. In a small German town, it worked immediately.

In each place, people suddenly turned into mindless, babbling creatures who thrashed about wildly, uttering weird, half-human cries – and then died a hideous death. Doctors and scientists were baffled as to the cause. Was it a sudden epidemic, an unknown virus?

But to the members of the United Network Command for Law and Enforcement, there could only be one answer: THRUSH had discovered a deadly new weapon for world conquest.

B☒XTREE

OTHER PAPERBACK TITLES
AVAILABLE FROM BOXTREE

NOVELS

☐ 1-85283-877-9	*The Man From U.N.C.L.E.*	£3.99
☐ 1-85283-882-5	*The Man From U.N.C.L.E.*	
	The Doomsday Affair	£3.99
☐ 1-85283-791-8	*The Prisoner: I Am Not A Number!*	£3.99
☐ 1-85283-830-2	*The Prisoner: Who Is No. 2?*	£3.99

REFERENCE

☐ 1-85283-260-6	*The Prisoner and Dangerman*	£14.95
☐ 1-85283-244-4	*The Complete Avengers*	£12.99
☐ 1-85283-141-3	*The Incredible World of 007*	£15.99
☐ 1-85283-164-2	*Thunderbirds Are Go!*	£9.99
☐ 1-85283-191-X	*Stingray*	£9.99
☐ 1-85283-277-0	*The Encyclopedia of TV Science Fiction*	£19.99
☐ 1-85283-129-4	*The Boxtree Encyclopedia of*	
	TV Detectives	£17.99

All these books are available at your local bookshop or newsagent, or can be ordered direct from the publisher. Just tick the titles you want and fill in the form below.

Prices and availability subject to change without notice.

Boxtree Cash Sales, P.O. Box 11, Falmouth, Cornwall TR10 9EN.

Please send cheque or postal order for the value of the book, and add the following for postage and packing:

U.K. including B.F.P.O. – £1.00 for one book, plus 50p for the second book, and 30p for each additional book ordered up to a £3.00 maximum.

Overseas including Eire – £2.00 for the first book, plus £1.00 for the second book, and 50p for each additional book ordered.

OR please debit this amount from my Access/Visa Card (delete as appropriate).

Card Number ☐☐☐☐☐☐☐☐☐☐☐☐☐☐☐☐☐☐

Amount £ ....

Expiry Date ....

Signed ....

Name ....

Address ....